PENGUIN BOOKS

THE
Yellow
VILLA

Amanda Hampson grew up in rural New Zealand. She spent her early twenties travelling, finally settling in Australia in 1979 where she now lives in Sydney's Northern Beaches. Writing professionally for more than 20 years, she is the author of two non-fiction books, numerous articles and novels *Two for the Road*, *The Olive Sisters* and *The French Perfumer*.

THE *Yellow* VILLA

AMANDA HAMPSON

PENGUIN BOOKS

PENGUIN BOOKS

UK | USA | Canada | Ireland | Australia
India | New Zealand | South Africa | China

Penguin Books is part of the Penguin Random House group of companies
whose addresses can be found at global.penguinrandomhouse.com.

Penguin
Random House
Australia

First published by Penguin Random House Australia Pty Ltd, 2018
This edition published by Penguin Random House Australia Pty Ltd, 2019

Cover design by Nikki Townsend Design
Cover photograph courtesy of Villa Marguerite and Les. Ladbury/Alamy Stock Photo
Typeset in Adobe Garamond by Midland Typesetters, Australia
Printed and bound in Australia by Griffin Press, an accredited ISO AS/NZS 14001
Environmental Management Systems printer.

A catalogue record for this
book is available from the
National Library of Australia

ISBN 978 0 14378 434 0

penguin.com.au

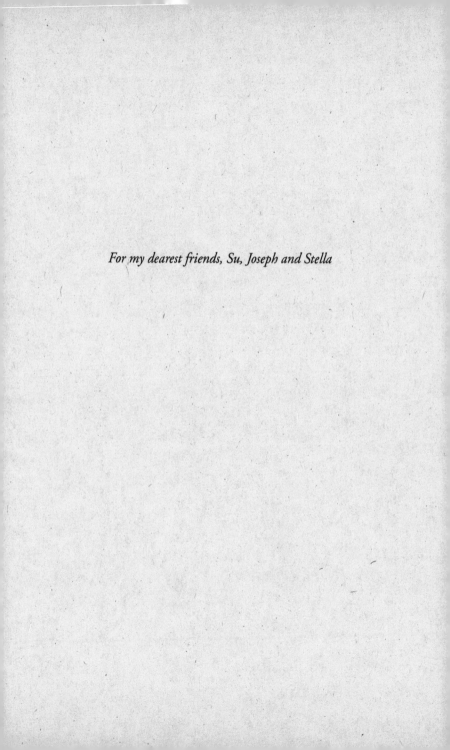

For my dearest friends, Su, Joseph and Stella

Chapter One

Each night I wake before midnight and wander the house. Even after a week in France, my body clock is bound to the opposite time zone and I have become more familiar with the house in darkness than in daylight. My feet follow the same route each night but my thoughts take a less direct path, retracing the steps that led me to this place, never sure if I made a conscious decision or was swept here as a result of being untethered. I should be thrilled. France was always my dream. What's not clear to me is how to live that dream in a practical sense. The attraction of a dream is its elusiveness; its elevation above the everyday.

When Ben and I arrived a week ago, we stayed the first couple of days in a nearby B&B, Le Bleu de Pastel, while we made our *maison* habitable. Long-haul flights are incubators for viruses and I soon felt the niggling throat, a thickening in the chest, every bone aching. Ben speaks almost no French so I had to accompany him to the various shops to gather essentials for the house, resisting the temptation of a soft bed in a dark and silent room.

Since we moved into the house, I have slept on and off all day, alternately feeling hot or cold or thirsty. Ben comes and goes like a faithful servant, waiting on me so sweetly. When I wake, it's either to the reassuring hum of his signature snore or to delicate birdsong from the garden and I know he has drawn the heavy curtains to shield me from the bright September day outside.

From the tall, graceful windows of our upstairs bedroom we can see the village of Cordes-sur-Ciel. By day, a sepia cluster of medieval houses crowded on a hilltop, by night a circlet of lights, white and gold, like a necklace dropped carelessly from the heavens. A waning moon has hovered over its shoulder these last few nights. In the early dawn, the hill is wreathed in cloud that sometimes enshrouds the house as well, setting us adrift in a sea of white.

As I walk the hallways, the boards creak cold under my feet, my fingers glance off the wall for balance, feeling the texture of the wallpaper. The house is too big for us – four times the size of our inner-city Sydney terrace. Seen online from the other side of the world, this house was the fairytale mansion with its ornate wrought-iron gates, wide gravel entrance and elegant proportions. The stone walls of the house are painted in a soft yellow with shutters in a darker shade: primrose and daffodil, or maybe sunflower and marigold. The setting, in a rural lane at the foot of the hill with a huge garden encircled by dry-stonewalls, looked idyllic. All this at half the price of our terrace. We hadn't planned this move. We had no plans. Ben made it happen. He did it for me. This was my dream, not his. He did it to save us.

My night-time wanderings have reduced the scale of the house to textures and details: the smoothness of the stone stairs, the burnished handrail, the cold metal lion's head on the newel post, the pinpricks of diffused light through the frosted glass of the double front doors.

Each night I stand in doorways and stare into the dark rooms, seeing only the shapes of the furniture in whatever light the moon gives up, wondering about the lives lived here. There's one room in particular that draws me, night after night. It's there I stand the longest. I know I should be thinking about practical things but my thoughts are too scattered to even try.

In the early hours, the wind comes up. It slips under the front doors, rattles around every window frame and whistles up through the attic and I return to my bed.

This property was *la propriété du défunt* – a deceased estate. I think about the old lady who lived here, Madame Levant, who stipulated in her will that it be sold to a young couple. It wasn't until we took possession that the *notaire* revealed this clause. We're in our mid-thirties, not that old but not that young either. It seems we unwittingly slipped through a loophole. I believe that Madame Levant wanted a young couple who would fill these rooms with the sounds of children. That will not be us. That can never be us.

Over the last few days, the house explored in the dreaming hours has become more familiar to me. I feel a growing affection for the odd creaks and sighs and shifting shadows. The dawn breeze seems to slow and thread itself through the house as if enfolding us, and no longer buffeting against us.

Today I woke to sunlight, the curtains pushed open. I have slept through the midnight hours and woken in time to see the pattern of morning sun as it falls on the Turkish rug beside the bed. After days of darkness and shadow, the colours seem bright as precious stones – sapphire, ruby, emerald and topaz – and the sky outside a wash of translucent blue. It's time to join the land of the living. Or, at the very least, my husband.

Chapter Two

Susannah Harrington stands in front of her full-length mirror and inspects herself from all angles. She's chosen a dark-blue sundress that complements her eyes and highlights the last traces of blonde in her hair, disguising the undergrowth of grey stealthily taking charge. Long and thick, it's still her best feature and a welcome distraction from the fretwork of lines encroaching on a face once considered by many to be beautiful. Although thickened with age and lacking its former pertness (everything seems to need shoring up these days), this dress flatters her figure.

She pulls on a cream cardigan. Takes it off. Drapes it over her shoulders. Tilts her head left and right, adds a smile and is satisfied it achieves the casual *élan* she desires. Lou-Lou and Chou-Chou sit at her feet and gaze adoringly at her reflection in the mirror. 'Does Mummy look pretty?' she asks, kneeling to bestow a kiss on each of the pug's soft little heads. 'Not as pretty as you, my little poppets.'

Susannah has been planning to visit the new arrivals as soon as courtesy allowed. Just over a week has elapsed, which seems about right. This afternoon she and Dominic will summon whatever tatters of charisma they still possess (something they'd once had in spades) and make themselves known. Of course, Dominic knows nothing of these plans and strategies and his cooperation can never be relied on.

In the interim, she has discovered that the new neighbours are an Australian couple with the endearing name of Tinker. Mia and Ben Tinker. Young enough to be the Harringtons' offspring but Susannah hasn't wasted a moment worrying whether they will find anything in common with a couple so much younger – she will make it work. One simply needs to take a real interest in people, since almost no one does these days.

She hasn't actually spied the Tinkers themselves but, passing on her way to the village, she has noticed the property is a hive of industry. The pair of evil-eyed billy goats that guarded the place have disappeared. Their droppings, which had long encrusted the front steps, have been scrubbed away. A van from a furniture store in Albi was sighted earlier in the week delivering appliances and mattresses. A telephone technician from Orange had been there practically every day, quite an accomplishment in itself, given the procurement of any kind of trade or service is at best torturous and at worst impossible.

Susannah puts on her glasses and peers into the mirror to apply her lipstick. Sadly, even her mouth, once so generous and giving, is beginning to look mean-spirited: the corners tending to droop, giving her a begrudging look. It's as though something inside her is receding, becoming diminished. Loneliness has a way of surreptitiously telegraphing itself like a disagreeable illness. There's something faintly repellant about it. That's not something she wants the Tinkers to pick up on. So, today she will play the part of the interesting, sophisticated older woman. The only role left to her now.

When she and Dominic first arrived in Cordes, a year ago, a veritable flotilla of friendships had sailed their way. They were just the sort of fresh 'interesting' new arrivals that established expats welcomed. Several of them were involved with the town theatre, and she had envisaged a quiet resurgence of her acting career. But one by one those friendships capsized. Now it's just her and Dominic again, alone with each other.

In the living room, the man himself is engrossed in the latest issue of *Decanter* and reluctant to be roused from his armchair. 'Who are these people?' he asks, without looking up.

'Darling, the yellow house on rue Albert Bouquillon, I told you . . .'

'With half the trades in the Tarn queued up outside. Probably Russian mafia.'

'You've always wanted to see inside the house, you said . . .'

'Yes, but why today?' He glances up from his magazine briefly as though he's on a deadline to finish it. 'And why are you all dolled up?'

'Just humour me, please. It's a beautiful afternoon. We can take the dogs and walk down.'

With an exasperated sigh, Dominic puts down his magazine, slugs his drink and pushes himself out of his armchair. 'I gather there's an expectation that I will also don my finery for this auspicious occasion? Who are we playing? Bogart and Bacall?'

'I've laid out a couple of suggestions on your bed. Come on, we need to get out.'

'Suggestions? Alternatives, you mean. I have no need *whatsoever* to get out. You're imposing *your* need on me.'

Susannah smiles. Today her benevolence works. With a commensurate amount of huff and distant mutterings, he changes his clothes and breezes out the front door, leaving her and the dogs to follow in a slipstream of expensive eau de cologne.

Rue Albert Bouquillon, despite its illustrious name, is a narrow country lane. It runs parallel to their own road with their house set back behind the Tinkers' property, down a gravel side road leading deeper into the countryside. It could be accessed cross-country via ploughed fields and a small wood, but the road is more reliable and a pleasant stroll.

Thankfully Dominic's mood improves as they walk. Today is perfect for their visit. A golden afternoon, typical of late September in South West France, the sun just beginning its descent beyond the hill, the air soft and shadows lengthening – if only one could add a soundtrack to these pivotal moments in life. The dogs are excited to be out and off their leashes. They run ahead, stopping now and then to glance back, making sure they are not alone. Quite the family occasion. There's every reason for optimism.

As they approach the house, Susannah once again admires the gracefulness of this sleeping beauty, now being brought back to life. The tall wrought-iron gates that culminate in a fanciful knot of curves and flowers and leaves; the wide front steps dividing the perfect symmetry of the building and the lovely little Juliet balcony above the front doors with double shuttered windows either side. It's been empty so long, it still has the neglected air of an abandoned property, like so many in France these days.

Mia Tinker opens the door to them. Wearing workman's overalls, dark hair cropped short, she's petite and lovely in the careless, unselfconscious way of young women everywhere.

She seems a little pale and disoriented but explains that she's been unwell and this is her first day out of bed. Nevertheless, she's welcoming and delighted to meet English speakers and fusses over Lou and Chou in the manner of a true dog lover. Susannah suggests they come back another day, but Mia is insistent they must come inside and meet Ben.

Susannah's first impression of the interior is of its understated beauty. Facing west, the gilded afternoon light floods the vestibule, illuminating the intricate floor tiling, the elegance of the curving stone staircase and the splendid high ceilings. No showiness, just perfect bones.

'Always been curious about the interior of this place,' admits Dominic, looking around. 'You're both Australian, then?'

'Yes, we are.' Mia smiles. 'Escapees from the colonies.'

'We love Australians!' declares Susannah, over-compensating with, 'So down to earth and super friendly. Super people!'

Ben comes down the stairs, solid but fit and strong looking, an archetypal Australian male to Susannah's eyes. The sort of man in whom you can still see the boy. With a cursory wipe of his grubby hand on his shorts, he shakes their hands enthusiastically. 'Welcome! English speakers. Excellent.'

'We've brought you a welcome gift,' says Dominic, handing Ben a bottle of wine. Although he's appreciative, Susannah can tell that this young man has no idea of its value. Admittedly, neither has she, but would hazard a guess that it's over the hundred-euro mark, knowing Dominic.

'We were so pleased to hear the new owners were *anglais* – not that we make a habit of seeking out expats, of course. We're not *those* sorts of expats,' says Susannah, already annoyed with herself for gushing.

'You may know that this style of house is what's called *une maison de maître*: the master's house, or perhaps more commonly called a villa these days, a more opulent style than the village houses,' explains Dominic. 'They can run to eight or ten bedrooms or more, with extensive grounds, orchards and stables.'

'We think five is more than enough,' says Mia with a nervous laugh.

'Probably built for someone of note in the late 1800s; I believe it was in Madame Levant's family for several generations.' Dominic looks around, nodding his head approvingly. 'Nice features. Very nice.'

'We're just about to stop for the day, will you stay for a glass of wine?' asks Ben.

'We really don't want to put you to any bother,' says Susannah.

As usual, Dominic has other ideas. 'Actually, now we've made it in the door, I wouldn't mind a tour of the place.'

Since the Tinkers seem amenable, Susannah capitulates. 'Oh, well, perhaps just a small glass of something. We truly only planned to pop our heads in.'

As they set off on the tour, Susannah notices how pretty the interior is. The downstairs walls are painted in a pale butter colour adding warmth to these huge rooms. It hasn't been maintained in the few years since the old lady died but is in a reasonable state, lacking ostentation but not entirely austere. The front rooms are a formal dining room and a large salon, both with vast stone fireplaces that will be difficult to clean. There are bits and pieces of furniture left behind; Madame Levant must have sold off the better pieces. There's a tatty crimson velvet chaise, various Louis XV-style chairs, the odd cabinet and side table scattered about and a formal dining suite that would easily seat a dozen for dinner. All have seen better days and none of it is worth very much in France. There may be a gem tucked away in a corner but most likely Madame had a dealer through the place some years ago. The parquet floors of the main salon need re-polishing; the blue jacquard curtains that dress the tall windows are faded, their gold tassel tie-backs hanging limp and thin as corn silk. What the salon lacks in grandeur it makes up in the aesthetic of its proportions.

Susannah takes it all in and makes the occasional comment about the views or the lovely light in each room. Dominic asks practical questions about the heating and plumbing. Ben admits that, since the weather is still so warm, they haven't yet put the radiators to the test. Installing the internet has apparently been the main priority but he's concerned about the electricity cutting out intermittently.

The rear of the ground floor has a long reception room with one entire wall of French windows that open out into the garden. The only furnishings are a refectory table and a variety of mismatched chairs. Off this room, a short hallway with a couple of small utility rooms, one being a butler's pantry, the other a storage room that leads to a spacious kitchen in the north-east corner. The kitchen has the original marble worktops, polished timber cupboards, a smaller table and chairs and a combustion fire that will be cosy in the winter.

'You're very lucky to have an intact kitchen,' says Susannah. 'In France people pack up their kitchen and take it with them. Such a nuisance.'

Mia gazes around the room. 'We love all this old furniture. Just the whole style of it. It would have taken us months to furnish the place.'

'I expect you'll get rid of a lot of it,' says Dominic. 'Other people's junk . . .'

'You never know what you might find in a house this age,' says Susannah.

'Hundred-year-old junk, is still, by definition, junk,' Dominic points out.

'Well, we're not in any rush,' says Mia. 'We're just exploring room by room.'

Having looped around the downstairs rooms, they come full circle to the entry vestibule, and continue up the main staircase to the first floor. Susannah picks up Lou and is touched to see Mia pick up Chou and carry her up the stairs.

'So . . . when did you actually see the property?' asks Susannah. 'It's been for sale ever since we arrived in Cordes a year ago.'

'Actually, we noticed it four years ago. We came here to Cordes-sur-Ciel on our honeymoon,' explains Ben. 'We stayed at the B&B Le Bleu de Pastel for a few days. It was summer then and we came for a walk down rue Albert Bouquillon one evening.'

'It was for sale back then. We loved the place; it seemed so sad and neglected. We came again in the daytime to get a better look but didn't have time to arrange a viewing,' says Mia.

'Or even seriously consider buying it,' adds Ben.

'Then, earlier this year, Ben looked online and saw it was still for sale . . . we made an offer and . . .' Mia shrugs as if she doesn't quite understand what happened. 'It's as though it was here waiting for us.'

'You can just buy a house over the internet?' Susannah is constantly dazzled by the scope of this new world.

Mia smiles. 'You can find one, at least.'

'It was kind of a spontaneous purchase. A mad experiment,' says Ben.

Intrigued, Susannah wonders what the objective of this experiment might be. Obviously the beginning of a new chapter, but what happened at the end of the last one? 'It was meant to be,' she agrees. 'Congratulations to you both.'

The upstairs bedrooms are decorated with floral wallpapers and dark furnishings from early last century but are wonderfully spacious with high ceilings and tall windows that look over the countryside of green fields, hedgerows and woods stretching off into the distance. The back bedrooms look towards the Harringtons' property; the front ones have a perfect view of the village on the hill.

'You've got an awful lot done in a short time. I'm amazed you even managed to get the EDF to connect the power so quickly,' says Susannah.

'We've had some help along the way. Plus Ben is a brilliant planner. He's the master of the spreadsheet; nothing's left to chance.'

The men go down to the basement to inspect the boiler and Susannah follows Mia to the kitchen where she sets about locating four glasses and a corkscrew, preparing to open the bottle brought by the Harringtons.

'Oh, please, don't open this on our account. I can duck home for a bottle of plonk if need be. Don't waste it on us.'

Mia looks up in surprise. 'I have other wine . . . I just thought . . .'

'Dominic's a collector, a connoisseur. Sorry – that sounds so horribly pretentious.' Susannah gives an embarrassed laugh. 'But truly, you should save it for a special occasion. Or a rainy day.

There won't be rainy days. The sun will shine eternal. Take no notice of me.' She pulls herself up short. 'By the way, whatever happened to those awful goats?'

'We still have them. They're not so bad.' Mia opens a bottle of white wine from the fridge and fills a bowl with water for the dogs, who are panting noisily.

'I was always terrified of the beasts. Vicious horns. Someone left the gates open once and they terrorised the entire neighbour-hood, eating people's washing and chasing the children.'

'They're quite secure now. We've got them running on a wire up the back, eating up the grass.'

'This is a nice big room – kitchen table's not bad,' says Susannah, pulling up a chair. 'Mixed blessing, inheriting bits of Madame Levant's old furniture. The French have rather odd taste in furniture . . .' Susannah glances at Mia. 'Oh, I didn't mean . . .'

Mia laughs. 'I do know what you mean. As I said, we like old things.'

'You're very enterprising and you obviously have good French, out buying fridges and beds and whatnot.'

'I learned French as a child, but Ben is struggling. He's been trying to learn; it's not easy.'

'He will, he's young. You're very practical, the two of you.'

Mia pours two glasses of wine. 'I'm not sure you could call buying this place practical. I wake in the night wondering if I've dreamed it.'

'I know what you mean. I had the same experience when we arrived. I wasn't sure if I even liked the house. Dominic was mad about the cellar. I did love the swallows nesting in the eaves . . . sounds silly, doesn't it? I've never told Dominic that, he would think it ridiculous. I just thought . . . they mate for life, swallows, don't they. It seemed a good omen.' Susannah abruptly lifts her glass in a toast. 'Here's to the great enterprise! *Bon courage!*' Their eyes meet as they clink glasses, and Susannah asks, 'Have you met any of the other local expats?'

'We really haven't had a moment. I hadn't thought of us as expats. Aren't we migrants?'

'I suppose you're right. I've always thought of myself as an expat. I'll never be French.'

'So, would you move back to England?'

'In a heartbeat.' Susannah surprises herself with a brittle laugh. 'Sorry. Take no notice of me. Of course not, we love it here. Besides, we couldn't really afford to go back. Even if we wanted to.'

Of course she'd love to go home, and she wonders for the thousandth time if there will ever come a day when they can show their faces in London again.

Chapter Three

The morning after their meeting with the Harringtons, Ben wakes to the realisation that his sense of displacement has eased slightly. He's never been someone who needs people around him all the time, but he had already begun to feel isolated. He prides himself on being a man who develops, strategises and considers all aspects of a situation. In a teasing mood, Mia calls him Dot-Point Boy. Colleagues often rib him about his 'listamania' and 'spreadsheetitus'. Planning, he often hears himself explaining, is not the same as procrastination – it's due diligence. It helps avoid mistakes. But there was little forethought or planning in his uncharacteristically impractical proposal to buy a house in France. It was purely emotional, driven by desperation. He knew it would instinctively appeal to Mia, the more impulsive, adventurous one. That was as far as his plan went.

Now here they are in this large, dusty house filled with furniture left behind by a dead stranger. Every morning he wakes disoriented, as though his ponderous self is lagging behind the new reality created by his spontaneous self. Every day he reminds himself that geographical location is irrelevant, Mia is home for him, and she will always be. His heart knows this to be the truth but his head is still bumbling around, trying to come to grips with it all. He resists contemplating the countless disadvantages of living in France for him. Feeling displaced is natural. That's why he needs to hold firm to the here and now.

He liked Dominic right away. He reminds Ben a little of his dad who was also taciturn and easily irritated. His dad is a long time gone: twenty years since his death. Memories of him have slowly diminished, fading and losing clarity. Maybe that's why Dominic seems oddly familiar.

Today Ben plans to set up his work station in the smaller of the back bedrooms and let his team leader know he's online and ready to join the new project. Starting work will normalise things. The virtual world is a constant. Right now it's the lack of structure he's finding difficult to navigate. He feels a rush of enthusiasm for this plan. About to roll out of bed, he hesitates, pausing to watch Mia sleep.

Her breathing is low and soft. She wears a gentle smile, a sight that never fails to bring a slight contraction to his heart. This time he must stay alert. He's sure that his absorption with work was a factor in everything that went wrong. More than anything, in his new iteration, he wants to be awake to everything. To look out the window just for the pleasure of the scene beyond. To step outside and feel the air. His natural tendency has always been to bury himself in work. When he was studying, he'd worked part-time with a landscaping firm, often toiling on properties with views only the ridiculously rich could afford. It was only later that he realised how seldom he looked up from the work, instead focusing entirely on the task, registering the weather in absolutes: hot, cold, wet, dry. Now he is determined to be open to nuance, to develop his finer senses.

Mia murmurs something inaudible, turns on her side, away from him. He edges across and tucks his knees behind hers, shelters her within his body. She half rolls towards him and gives him a sleepy kiss that makes him glad he didn't follow his first instinct to get up and start work. He slides his hand across her belly and she wriggles into his arms, entwines her legs with his. This is something new, something he thought they had lost forever, something he had yearned for when it all fell apart. But here she is, embracing him, welcoming him home. He feels a sting of tears. Relief. Gratitude.

Chapter Four

In the sanctuary of his study, Dominic finds it impossible to concentrate on his reading with the unholy racket that Susannah insists on making all over the house; a discordant symphony of slamming doors and cupboards interspersed with the wheeze and drone of the hoover. The problem persists that the woman possesses no organisational talents whatsoever. No concept of time and motion. It would never enter her mind to systematically clean one room at a time or hoover the whole house in one sweep. She persistently starts one thing and then becomes distracted by another, undertaking multiple tasks simultaneously – and none of them terribly well. Most infuriating is her habit of leaving the hoover in the middle of the living room for a week, arguing that she hasn't finished. By the time she gets back to the bloody thing, it's time to start again.

Dominic abandons his book (A.A. Gill's memoir, an exhausting read at the best of times) and indulges himself with a finger of Scotch and warm memories of bygone days when they could afford help. Their last housekeeper had been a Polish woman who belted through the place like Napoleon taking Austerlitz, marshalling the house into a state of cleanliness, terrorising everything in her path. He admired her rigid strategy: she did the entire house in precisely the same order every week. No good expecting that kind of efficiency from Susannah. He probably should have married a Polish peasant instead of a pampered prima donna. He closes his eyes and visualises the anatomy of Madame Gomolka. On reflection, she was built like a wrestler: compact and somewhat rectangular, likely the genetic inheritance of generations of pickaxe-wielding females. Lacking allure, certainly, but perhaps that was a small price to pay for having one's house running at peak efficiency. He abhors mess. Anyhow, there is something to be said for Susannah actually cleaning the place in preparation for the visit from their new young friends. Usually her idea of preparation is faffing about filling every blasted vase with flowers and rearranging cushions and whatnot.

It is some time since they've entertained and he feels a cosy sense of anticipation. Fresh blood and all that. Of course, he has his own preparations to attend to, selecting the tipple for the evening. He toys with the idea of something local, perhaps the Gaillac Chateau de Laven. Not too pricey but guaranteed to impress even the most uneducated antipodean palate.

Despite his best efforts to avoid her, Susannah intercepts him en route to the cellar, announcing: 'I'll go to the market shortly. I'm doing *poulet à la provençale* and *crème brûlée*.'

'Dear God, can't we do better than that? We might as well take them to the bar in the village.'

'Dominic. We don't want to intimidate them. They'll be terrified to invite us back.'

'You must think highly of your culinary prowess if you really think a decent cassoulet would strike terror into their hearts.'

'I want to make them feel comfortable,' insists Susannah. 'At home.'

'Why not make them feel entirely at home with a barbecue or Vegemite soldiers? Shouldn't we give them something to aspire to?' Dominic gives a sigh and capitulates, 'Oh, do whatever you want. Unlike you, I obviously haven't developed an entire strategy around the event.'

'I want them to like us. They're so lovely. Young idealists.'

'Dreamers, you mean. The cost of heating that place in the winter . . . it'd be cheaper to shut it up and fly back to Australia first class. I'll be surprised if they last the winter.'

'Well, considering you have such a negative opinion, they seem to have put you in a good frame of mind.'

'All these years and you still can't differentiate negativity from pragmatism. Not sure about her but I liked him a lot,' admits Dominic. 'He's got a lot of youthful energy. Focus and passion.'

'Now you're going to tell me that he reminds you of yourself at that age.'

'Is that because I'm a narcissist who can only appreciate reflections of myself? Anyway, you didn't even know me then. I was on fire. A man's in his prime in his thirties. Brimming with ideals and passions. Even an old sourpuss like me. Actually, I'm planning on taking the lad under my wing. He has the French of a newborn: grunt and point. How's he possibly going to manage?'

'He seems to be doing all right so far. Besides, Mia obviously speaks decent French. What I'm saying is . . . as long as you're kind to him . . . to them both.'

'Yes, yes . . . obviously, why would I be unkind? You evidently think me a complete boor incapable of being pleasant to people.'

'Not incapable, just unwilling sometimes. They're wholesome and charming . . .'

'How many inane adjectives can you possibly dredge up to describe two ordinary people? Besides they're *straylians* – they don't share our national obsession with manners. Very refreshing too. Didn't we leave England to get away from all that nonsense?'

'Dominic. Now you're being absolutely ridiculous. You know perfectly well that's not true. And on that topic, please don't let them find out about that. Don't drop any hints, just stay off the topic altogether.'

'Anything else? Any further directives?'

'All I'm saying is, we don't know how much is on the internet for someone who wants to find it. So don't leave any crumbs for them to follow . . .'

'Aren't you getting a bit ahead of yourself? A mere second ago you were waxing lyrical about their wholesome loveliness, now you're worried they're going to start stalking us?'

'Dominic! People can just look things up on the internet. They don't consider it stalking. It's called being "informed" . . . or googling . . . or whatever . . .'

Infuriatingly, Susannah views the internet with a childlike wonder, believing it a storybook wardrobe through which one can enter a magical hidden world. She's the clichéd primitive, baffled by the sight of the giant silver bird spilling its vapour trail overhead. She used to be intelligent. The twenty-first century has rendered her stupid and he fervently wishes, for both their sakes, that she would desist from commenting on modern technology altogether.

'For Christ's sake . . .' he barks, startling the slumbering pugs who look up with the plaintive expressions of children fearing an impending divorce. Suddenly weary of the argument, Dominic realises he's quite forgotten exactly what he felt so strongly about only moments earlier. Before Susannah can get going on another topic, he makes his escape to the cold silence of the cellar. His nirvana. A place where he feels completely at one with the world.

Built under the kitchen, the cellar comprises a series of brick tunnels making it soundproof to such an extent that it feels as though one is wearing earplugs. A sort of sensory deprivation experience. When they first viewed the cottage as a potential bolthole, the cellar was the major selling point for him. Naturally an ideal temperature for wine storage, always cool and dry, with the house above insulating it from extremes of heat and cold. It was an expensive exercise to ship his wine collection over from England but truly a joy to behold all his precious bottles nestled snugly in their purpose-built racking.

As he inspects the troops, pulling out a bottle here and there, considering it and replacing it, he recalls Mia's comment about the house waiting for them. At the time he'd dismissed it as typical of that generation's self-absorbed magical thinking but now it occurs to him that he felt something similar about this cellar. Most rural French houses have cellars; he and Susannah had seen dozens in their search. Damp, smelly holes many of them – one half expected to find the remains of some poor sod held captive since the war, or a kidnap victim whose ransom remained unpaid. But this cellar is a thing of beauty: half the footprint of the house and crafted with both artisan skill and a fine aesthetic sense. He must bring

Ben down to inspect it; he's sure to have an appreciation of the finer structural elements. In fact, he'll introduce the boy to some wines – undertake to educate his palate. Now, there's a project! Susannah is right about one thing: the Tinkers are terribly sweet. Although too much sweetness can be cloying. It's a little saltiness that adds depth and flavour.

Chapter Five

We walk down the rue Albert Bouquillon towards the Harringtons' house in a creamy dusk. Clouds of rose and violet drift across the pale evening sky. We walk in silence, each lost in our own thoughts. My hand rests lightly in the crook of Ben's arm and I can almost imagine us as an elderly couple, a little bowed and grey, our lives behind us. What troubles me, not just now but often, is the more existential question of what our lives will have been about. Will we feel satisfied with the lives we've led? Or will we have simply gone through the motions? I often wonder if other people think about this as much as I do. Many people seem content to lead lives of routine and habit, never reaching beyond the everyday to find something more fulfilling. I wish I could be one of them. I truly do. The thought of us growing old gives me an odd empty feeling as though time is accelerating and our lives are almost over with nothing worthwhile achieved. I wonder what can be truly meaningful in a life without children, and still no answers appear.

An older woman wearing a black coat and brown hat passes us, walking in the opposite direction. I smile and nod. '*Bonsoir, Madame.*' Ben murmurs something inaudible. His confidence is a bit bruised by the less-than-enthusiastic response towards his French from the locals.

'*Messieurs-dames.*' The woman bobs her head and gives us a curious side glance.

When she has passed, I ask Ben if he's seen her before. She looks familiar to me.

He glances over his shoulder briefly. 'Nah.'

'I think I remember seeing her standing at the gates . . . as though she wanted to come in. I remember the hat.' I turn around and see that the woman has paused outside our house. She sees me watching and hurries away up the road.

Clusters of tiny magenta cyclamen grow wild alongside the Harringtons' laneway. The sight of them draws my thoughts back to the beauty of the evening around us, the sounds of birdsong and smell of woodsmoke. It's hard to imagine that the novelty of walking to dinner along these peaceful country lanes and returning home by the light of a torch could ever wear off.

The Harringtons' house is set about half a kilometre across the fields behind ours but it's much easier to access by a road that leads away from the village. The two-storey farmhouse stands on its own surrounded by fields. A stone wall encloses a courtyard with a few out-buildings attached, one of which has a dusty silver Audi parked in it.

The little pugs bark excitedly as Susannah welcomes us at the door and ushers us into a hall cluttered with umbrellas, boots and coats for all seasons hung along a row of hooks. She takes us into Dominic's study, which looks out into the front courtyard.

He gets up to greet us from behind a polished timber desk dominated by a large electric typewriter. The neat bookshelf, French impressionist prints on the wall and a couple of leather armchairs give it the timeless feel of one of those exclusive London clubs. The living room is also furnished in a conservative English style with antiques and florals, and an open fire, exactly as I had envisioned for the Harringtons.

'I've selected a little something from my small collection for this evening,' says Ben, handing Dominic back his gift.

'Ahh, the antipodean sense of humour.' Dominic smiles, accepting the wine from him.

'Sorry, it is a bit rude,' I say. 'We wanted to enjoy it with you . . . also we haven't had time to get out.' Ben figured this was the simple way to meet Dominic's wine expectations.

Dominic gazes fondly at the label. 'Don't apologise, I'm more than happy to have this little pony return to the stable. We might just save it for a special occasion. In fact, come down and see my cellar before it gets too dark . . .'

'They've scarcely got in the door, Dominic,' says Susannah.

Ben reassures her that we would like to see the cellar and we all make our way out through the sort of conservatory that leads off the living room into the garden. Outside is a pergola, like an archway entwined with roses, with a bench seat built into it. Like a romantic English garden.

'Dom wanted this house because of the cellar,' explains Susannah. 'But it was this lovely arbour that sold me. I adore roses. I've put in several of my favourite English tea roses to add more variety, so there's white as well as pink and peach —'

'It's something of an obsession for Susannah,' interrupts Dominic, and beckons us towards a path that leads along the back of the house. When I realise that Susannah isn't joining us, I offer to help her in the kitchen but she waves me off, insisting she'll attend to the dinner.

The cellars are tucked neatly under the house and accessed through a big alcove furnished with a rustic dining table and chairs. Dominic explains that this area is beautifully cool in summer and still has the original bread oven, which they use occasionally.

He unlocks the heavy steel door that leads into the cellar itself. 'I had this security door installed. I have some very rare vintages. One can never be too careful. Only problem is if the bloody thing slams, it deadlocks and you need the key to get out. I locked myself in here once; fortunately Susannah noticed me missing at supper-time. I keep an extra key in here now, just in case.'

He props the door wide open and switches on the lights. It's like a series of two or three tunnels, interesting but creepy at the same time. I don't like these sorts of enclosed spaces, especially ones with slamming doors, and find myself glancing anxiously at the hook inside the doorway where the spare key hangs. I know it's silly, I'm a grown woman and it's not as though he's going to lock us in the cellar. But it has a dense, earthy smell like tobacco that conjures up visions of being buried alive. The walls seem to push in on us. But much as I desperately want to get out of here, I sense that Dominic would think . . . I don't know what he'd think, but nothing good, that's for sure. Not aware of my growing anxiety, Ben listens, arms folded, nodding and asking questions while Dominic expands on his collecting strat-egies, pulling out various bottles to show us. I move in close beside Ben, comforted by the proximity of his bulk and warmth. Intuitively, he enfolds me in his arms and hugs me close, resting his chin on my head and I am safe.

Chapter Six

Susannah ferries each individual soufflé ramekin nestled in a heavy oven glove to the table while Dominic opens a second bottle of wine.

'I don't know why you have to bring them out one at a time. Why not a tray, Susannah? Just for dramatic effect? You should know that Susannah was an actress – it will explain a lot.' He seems mildly amused, teasing more than criticising, so the expedition to the cellars was evidently a success.

Leaning over her dish, Mia sniffs the pungent smell of Gruyère. '*Soufflé au chou-fleur*?'

'Yes, well done,' says Susannah, bringing the final ramekin to the table. 'An old favourite.'

'My mother used to make it for us when we were children,' says Mia.

'Ah, cauliflower cheese,' says Ben. 'We had it too but with tasty cheese.'

Dominic looks from one to the other. 'Tasty cheese? Well, we're pleased it's hit the spot.'

'Is your mother French?' asks Susannah as she sits down, still a little flustered. '*Bon appétit*, everyone . . . careful, it's hot!'

'No, she's Dutch. That's how we qualify to live in the EU. Actually, we call this *bloemkool met kaassaus*.'

'So, are you members of the Australian squattocracy or are you expecting to make a living of some sort here?' asks Dominic.

'Diversity. That's our strategy. Multiple income strands,' says Ben. 'I work online anyway. We can both work online, but we're open to all possibilities.'

'I think it's wonderful. You're young and energetic,' says Susannah. 'Why not try something new?'

'You probably know that renovating these old houses involves one nasty surprise after another, and heating them is another story altogether,' says Dominic. 'Buying one is an act of sheer folly, in fact – that's why they're so cheap.'

'We quite like the house as it is, that sort of grand shabby chic. We're not planning a massive renovation; more of a preservation,' says Mia.

Not to be deterred, Dominic continues. 'Plumbing, electrical, you'll find it all needs doing. The French are quite cavalier about these things. We had live wires poking out of the walls – deathtraps for the amateur. We've been through it all, so more than happy to offer counsel.'

Susannah has a growing concern that Dominic is now determined to pursue this topic until the Tinkers reveal the full depths of their ignorance. Nothing less will do. He has been in a generous, expansive mood, but now he seems to be searching for a fissure in their self-confidence. As though sensing this, Mia changes the subject, asking what brought the Harringtons to France.

'Sort of semi-retirement, really. Roles had dried up for me,' explains Susannah, launching into the story she now has off pat. 'We didn't want to stay in London. France was cheaper than Dorset or anywhere nice outside London. We looked at the Côte d'Azur. Much too expensive.'

'And too many bloody Russians,' adds Dominic.

'Then the Dordogne, or Dordogneshire as they call it.' Susannah smiles. 'That's become quite expensive too. Friends recommended that we look at Cordes-sur-Ciel. Obviously a gorgeous part of the world, then we saw this house all tucked away and fell for the whole package. That was a year ago.'

'What did you do for a living, Dominic?' asks Ben.

Unable to resist any opportunity to be centrestage, Dominic hesitates only for the briefest moment before inviting the Tinkers to make a guess. Not wanting to sit through this excruciating process, Susannah gets up and briskly clears the dishes, even though they have barely finished, and rushes them back to the kitchen. This is exactly what she asked Dominic not to do. She expressly told him *not* to make himself a subject of curiosity. Now she suspects he's doing it to spite her.

From the kitchen, Susannah can hear Ben suggesting all sorts of wishful *Boy's Own* pursuits: race-car driver, airline pilot, architect, private detective, spy, double agent – urged on by Dominic's laughter and encouragement. At least it's restoring his good temper. Mia says nothing. She's the more observant one. When Ben runs dry, Mia asks if, perhaps, since Susannah was an actress, was he a director or producer? No. Lawyer? Doctor? Susannah begins to wonder if Mia might be pandering to his ego. Clever girl. He, of course, is thoroughly enjoying all this speculation, basking in a self-imposed air of mystery.

Returning to the dining room with the main course, Susannah carefully places a plate in front of each of them, giving it a practised tweak to show the dish off to its best advantage. She looks up to see Mia observing her with interest.

'Were you a chef?' asks Mia, turning to Dominic.

Although he shakes his head, he looks guarded.

'Restaurant owner? No . . . okay. A food writer . . . a restaurant critic?'

For a split second he looks crestfallen, disappointed to be unmasked, but then raises his glass in tribute to her powers of perception. 'How did you arrive at that conclusion?'

Mia shrugs modestly. Susannah suspects it's the way Dominic watches her when she serves a meal, as if he's assessing her for a hospitality certificate. Over the years she's got used to it. Besides, he has many more annoying habits than that.

'Well done, Mia-Cat,' says Ben admiringly. 'She's the smart one in the family.'

Dominic gives Mia a doubtful look and quickly wrestles the focus back to where it belongs. 'I was always interested in food and wine; an epicure from an early age. My favourite pastimes are eating and drinking. Never thought of making a career of it. For years I was an unknown news hack – did the odd column, standing in here and there. Had the chance to do some restaurant reviews, they gained a certain notoriety and the paper was virtually forced to give me my own column. And the rest is history.'

'History?' asks Mia.

'A figure of speech, *ma chère*. Although, all humility aside, I was highly regarded in my day. Perhaps the best . . .' Susannah catches his eye and he hesitates. Changing this subject will be difficult now but Dominic does make an effort. 'Ben, you mentioned you liked a merlot; you'll find this has similar plummy overtones.' He holds the bottle aloft, eyebrows raised expectantly at them both. Mia shakes her head, insisting she's not much of a drinker. Susannah gets up and goes to the cabinet to fetch Ben another wineglass.

'Did you wear disguises?' asks Mia. 'Like fake beards and glasses?'

'The ones with a nose attached to the glasses and eyebrows?' suggests Ben.

'No disguises required. Kept my face out of the press. My name was known but I made my bookings under pseudonyms, obviously.'

'What were some of the restaurants you reviewed? Perhaps we can find your reviews online?' asks Mia.

Susannah is not sure whether she let go of the glass involuntarily – perhaps a sort of survival mechanism – or dropped the thing deliberately, but she's as startled as the rest of the party to hear the explosion of crystal as it hits the terracotta tiles.

Dominic stares at the mess of smashed crystal on the floor. Unnerved by his calm silence, Susannah trips over herself to apologise. 'Oh, darling, I'm terribly sorry . . . I'm so clumsy . . . I'll clear it up. Ignore me, everyone. Keep talking.'

Dominic turns to their guests. 'Baccarat crystal. Belonged to my mother, a woman of impeccable taste. Worth about two hundred pounds each, I'd say. I inherited a full dozen. Now there are just three left intact.'

Mia and Ben sit in the now uncomfortable silence broken only by the sound of Susannah hurriedly brushing the remains into a dustpan while she frets that the Tinkers will make their excuses and escape.

'But, as Oscar Wilde so wisely opined,' continues Dominic evenly, 'the one charm of the past is that it is the past. Do we have another glass for Ben? Try and keep a firm grip on this one, *ma chérie.*'

Susannah brings a second glass and disposes of the breakage. The talk turns to more general things, Susannah steering the attention towards the Tinkers. Ben reveals that he works as a software engineer; a computer programmer.

'Ahhh . . . the ubiquitous *inter*net,' says Dominic. 'If you didn't clamber onboard when everyone else did you're standing on the shore watching that particular vessel sail away. For many, it's a speck in the distance now.'

'I don't know. Any idiot can use it and a lot do,' says Ben.

'I've a reasonable grasp on the technology,' says Dominic. 'Simply don't have the use for it.'

'Was that something you always wanted to do?' Susannah asks Ben. 'I'm not sure what's involved in computer programming, to be honest.'

'Not really – when I was a kid, I always thought I'd be a farmer. Then my dad was killed in an accident when I was fourteen and the farm had to be sold. I managed to finish school and went down to Sydney to do vet science and ended up doing software engineering instead. It's pretty good. Plenty of work in a growth industry. Better paid than farming and you get to stay dry. I like problem solving. Mia's the creative one.'

'I met Ben's sister, Olivia, at university,' explains Mia. 'We ended up sharing a house with some other students. Ben moved in with us, so that's how we got together. I was doing fine arts, textile design. Bit of a useless degree so I went on and did education training and became an art teacher.'

Susannah makes all the right noises but knows nothing about computer work and very little about art. Dominic could hardly be less interested but does make an effort to appear so. After dessert, Susannah suggests they adjourn to the living room for the cheese course.

Even though Ben is clearly struggling to focus and Mia has two bright-red spots on her cheeks like a painted doll, Dominic opens yet another bottle of wine. Oblivious to their guests' waning attention, he insists on availing them of the provenance of each cheese, directing their attention with his little finger in the most pretentious way as though he's the *maître fromager*. Ben swallows a series of yawns, Mia's lids droop, and it falls to Susannah to set their guests free and send them home.

After they leave, Susannah clears up the kitchen, turns on the dishwasher and switches off the lights. She had assumed that Dominic had gone straight to bed, but now, from the darkness of the living room, she sees he's outside, sitting in a deckchair, staring up at the sky and smoking one of his expensive cigars. From his relaxed posture it's obvious he's reached the point of intoxication she considers the embodiment of his higher self. It's the middle part of drunkenness when he is at his worst: unpredictable, uncensored and over-invested in his own opinions. In the latter stages, he mellows. It's as though the alcohol warms his soul and releases the reserves of kindness and generosity he has buried deep in there. She has no desire to join him. Far from it. More than anything she wants to get to her own room without further ado to ensure that the evening ends on a high note.

It all went well enough, apart from the smashed glass and Dominic boring them absolutely senseless about the blasted cheeses, but she felt on edge the whole time. She has stupidly already invested too much in them to completely relax. It makes no sense, really. Perhaps it's just her pitiful state of loneliness but it feels like more than that. It's as though both she and Dominic see a chance to straighten themselves out. A sort of second chance at a time when third and fourth chances have already failed. With all their other friendships, bridges have not so much been burned as disassembled, with no return possible.

She ushers Lou and Chou out the front door, watches them fondly as they squat for their final pee of the day, then bundles them into her room and locks the door behind her. By the time she emerges from her ensuite, face cleansed and thickly lathered with night cream, her babies have nestled into the duvet. They watch her every move, their eyes pools of empathy and trust. She loves these two so deeply, just seeing them cuddled up on the bed waiting for her almost brings her to tears.

She settles herself in bed and gazes around her room at the pieces of furniture, paintings and small decorative items that bring her comfort. She looks at them in exactly the same order every night. And when she wakes at some ungodly hour, she will go through this ritual again. It stops the panic rising and over-taking her. It connects her with the past and with people outside this house, outside this country. She always starts at the door, on the back of which hangs her cream silk robe, a gift from Daddy. To the left hangs a portrait of Susannah in her twenties, painted by her first husband, Maxwell, who, at that time, was a theatre set designer and is now a highly respected director. Truly the kindest man in the world. There isn't a day that passes that she doesn't regret how careless she was with that marriage. Just thinking of him brings her comfort.

On the dresser, in a silver vase, a bunch of dried red roses, the bouquet she received for her role as Helga in the West End production of *The Honey Tree*. Maxwell arranged for these to be preserved for her as a memento. Perhaps he had a premonition that, despite strong reviews, her career would falter and fade away from that point on. Nevertheless, not everyone can claim a West End performance. Next comes her mother's silver brush and mirror set with pearl inlay. Precious objects steeped in memories, they somehow ease the pangs of self-recrimination she suffers these days, the sleepless nights spent traversing her life, re-examining every turning point, every decision. Her decisions were often just thoughtless responses to circumstance with no sense of possible repercussions. She allowed others to make decisions for her until there were no choices left. Now she is here. It always comes back to that.

Meeting these young people, with their life and potential ahead of them, throws into sharp relief the dreadful realisation that her potential is all behind her now. She once had promise. Everyone said so. A promising debut. A promising actress. When does promise expire? When she was young, people turned towards her – she was at the centre of things. At some point they began to turn away. She became someone who had not lived up to her early promise. She has a vision of herself as a butterfly that folds itself back into its chrysalis; a sort of reverse metamorphosis. The dreams she once had have been worn away, eroded by the abrasions of life. Her potential squandered on worthless pursuits.

Chapter Seven

Out on the patio, Dominic enjoys a snifter of Rémy while savouring one of his last Spanish Rosados. He breathes a sigh of satisfaction as the woody flavour of the cognac melds with the leathery undertone of the cigar. Who knew when he would be able to procure any more of these? Perhaps they should relocate to Cuba. That would solve several problems at once.

He turns his gaze to the night sky. Enchanted by the firmament of stars above, he is struck by the realisation that he is undergoing some sort of renaissance; a reawakening. This renewed appreciation of his surroundings is a gift of the Tinkers. Even their surname has a mischievous twinkle to it. Their charming naïveté and romantic idealism is like a tonic and having something of a redemptive effect on him.

His current situation, which he considers unsatisfactory, bordering on untenable, is being reconfigured through their admiring eyes. Even his home, which has little to redeem it – apart from the cellar – he has to acknowledge is comfortably bolstered and upholstered by contrast to the derelict discomfort of Chez Tinker. The ease of his own existence is more evident when compared to the great burden they have taken on themselves. In fact, at one point in the evening, as though perceiving Susannah as the Tinkers did, he caught a fleeting glimpse of the remnants of her once luminous beauty, seeing her as burnished by time rather than simply decaying. Of course, they haven't witnessed the woman's decline from artless *ingénue* to the harpy she has become today. Nevertheless, it did him good to be reminded that it wasn't always so.

More astonishing is that he's experiencing a momentary softening of his attitude towards the French whom he generally considers bloody-minded beyond redemption. But it seems that the entire race can be viewed more charitably through the rainbow prism of Mia's loving gaze, and she has brainwashed her husband to feel the same way.

Mia is evidently infatuated with the French. At one point during the evening, she expressed disbelief at the contradictory phenomena that every year more than eighty million people visit France because they are besotted with all things French but at the same time condemn the French for being themselves and protecting these things that visitors so admire. It's as though she was born into a cult of Francophiles. Half-a-dozen times this evening he'd had the urge to make some cutting remark about the mind-bending frustrations of dealing with the French but managed to restrain himself. While there is hardly a subject he prefers to the enumeration of his ever-growing list of complaints about his adopted country, he will not be the one to dampen their enthusiasm. He will not be the one to disillusion them – he will leave that to the French themselves. He'll simply be there to commiserate when the Tinkers are roused from their dreamy slumber. They will learn the hard way.

Say what you will about the British, and even Australians, for that matter, they do attempt to be helpful, particularly when they are being paid to do so – otherwise known as 'customer service' these days. A foreign concept in France. The French feel no such impulse. The phrase *'C'est pas possible'* spills from French lips before you even finish explaining what you want – never considering that it might be eminently possible. The lowliest clerk has a laser-like ability to locate the tiny detail that allows him to send you packing. If there isn't a rule, he will improvise. Some poor sod, simply trying to complete a basic administrative task, finds himself throttled by red tape and forced to debate, cajole and convince some petty bureaucrat to do his or her job. The woman at La Poste fairly bristles if she sees you approach with a large parcel, as if you're going to demand she personally cycle to Britain with the bloody thing under her arm.

The little Tinkers view things simplistically. For Ben, who is not a French speaker and quite possibly will never be fluent, there will be myriad subtleties that he could never pick up on but Mia may be more sensitive to the disapproving little snubs the French specialise in.

In all honesty, what he enjoys most about the Tinkers is the reflection he sees of himself. The respect, even reverence, they showed towards his knowledge of wines. And his (quite rudimentary) knowledge of the provenance of the cheeses had obviously impressed them – until Susannah interrupted and insisted they leave, practically throwing them out of the house. The woman has become a social liability.

And the sacrifice of crystal was quite unnecessary. He may have been getting carried away in the moment and perhaps a trifle indiscreet. But, truly, was it so difficult to give him a warning look, a cautionary signal? Pushing these irritations aside, he turns his gaze once more to the night sky and tips back the last of his drink. Bliss. He envisions himself as a mentor sharing his knowledge, his wisdom, his understanding of the world, inducting Ben into the temple of epicurean pleasures, starting with cognac and cigars. The dawn of a new era. Thank God.

Chapter Eight

After almost a month in the house, the initial shock of the move is behind us and we find ourselves in a honeymoon phase. Every day we work together to make the house more habitable. We're falling in love with the village of Cordes-sur-Ciel and with our new home. It's only just beginning to feel as though it is actually ours. Ben and I seem to be more in tune with each other too. Can it be this simple? I'm instinctively suspicious of anything simple. Simplicity is so often an illusion.

The shadow of our recent separation – something I never thought could happen – and the confusion of everything surrounding it still hover at my shoulder. But here we are, skating across the surface of life, the sun shines bright and our world has a golden sheen.

Most evenings we walk up the hill to the village just as the tiny shops and artisan ateliers are closing for the night. The winding cobblestone streets are almost empty, the tourists and daytrippers have disappeared into buses or hotels. Although the evenings are becoming cooler, we sit *en plein air* at the café in

Place de la Halle and enjoy a glass of wine. From the hilltop, the countryside is a patterned carpet of tree-lined fields, patches of woodlands and the river Le Cérou winding off into the distance with the occasional house or chateau tucked away. When the sky is clear, the sunset stretches above us like a great silken banner, woven in scarlets and golds. Within minutes it dissolves like sugar fondant into the palest pink and honey colours, fading slowly to a silver twilight and then, holding hands, we wander down the hill to our new home.

We've been eating mix-up meals with fresh produce from the village market. The dense flavours remind us of everything we loved about France from our earlier trips. The luscious flavours of a ripe tomato, the sour crust of French camembert and the tenderness of *haricots verts* – thin green beans that never taste as good anywhere as they do here. The combination of fresh *chèvre* smeared on ripe figs and washed down with a *vin rouge* is almost sensual. Ben may be having a hard time with the language but the food makes up for a lot. We share our enjoyment, taking turns to groan with pleasure, lavishing praise on every bite. The Normandy butter tastes so *buttery*, the Brie de Meaux deliciously nutty and earthy like mushrooms, and Ben remarks that it's as though his tastebuds are on ecstasy, every mouthful a high. He eats almost anything; I'm the more discerning foodie. He's a jaffle kind of a guy. Two pieces of bread and whatever he can find in the fridge, squash it together in the press and wolf it down. He sees that as fuel but fully appreciates that what we're eating now is next level.

At the end of the day, exhausted by our labours, satiated by food, and often too much wine, we fall into bed and make love with a passion I don't ever recall, even in the early years of our relationship. It's like rebound sex, but with each other. The house seems to have reunited us but all that really matters is that we can somehow see our future together.

Ben has set up his workstation in a bedroom that looks over the back garden. From there he can keep an eye on those troublesome goats who seem determined to eat only things they can't quite reach. We both brought our core computer gear from home and have now purchased three large monitors; he uses two that sit side by side on a table that has become his desk.

Soon he will disappear into the virtual world of a project on the other side of the globe where his scrum master will become the main woman in his life. We're lucky that he can work remotely but I'm worried about what I will do with myself while he works. I'm fearful of being left to my own devices, having to confront my lack of direction.

I know that I don't need to rush around trying to find a creative endeavour, I just need to be open to it finding me, and I might as well be doing something practical in the meantime. So I start by cleaning out the two small utility rooms between the kitchen and the room that runs along the rear of the house. There are so many rooms in this house, we've had to give them names. We call the larger room at the front of the house the salon, and the one beside it is obviously the dining room, and this long one that opens to the garden we call the summer room. It will be a while before it lives up to its name.

The utility rooms are small and dark; the only natural light comes from a window in the hallway that leads to the kitchen. I assume they were used for storing food and as overflow from the kitchen. One of them has a sink and bench, the other is empty apart from a few boxes. The house had been given a basic clean, and all Madame Levant's personal things have gone apart from odd bits and pieces that someone probably thought would be useful.

The boxes in the utility room contain old kitchen utensils, some nice old coffee cups and plates; nothing of real interest apart from a doll with a china face, her blue glass eyes dull with age and hair in tufts. I also find a baby's rattle, some glass marbles, the handle of a skipping rope. I try to imagine the house in earlier times, full of life, with children running through the hallways. We often hear the sounds of children chattering as they pass on their way to school, otherwise it is completely silent in this house.

I take the toys up to the little bedroom that continues to mystify me. It has a child-sized bed with an armchair beside it, as if positioned for a bedtime story. The wallpaper is patterned with blossom sprigs and tiny birds. The curtains are a dusky pink with a matching canopy over the bed. It's not like a shrine or anything like that; there are no belongings left here. The question is, who could this child be? Madame Levant apparently had no descendants, so presumably she had no grandchildren or great-grandchildren. Maybe this room was her childhood room, and remained as it was for almost a century. I sense there's something sad about it, as though it is more empty than other rooms.

I wash down the floors and the walls of the little store rooms. That's a simple job; the next will be to tackle the kitchen which needs a lot more work. Hopefully, we'll do that together. Working alone, I find my thoughts more in the past than the future. It's as though I have reached a roadblock and have to keep turning back in my search for the way forward.

Ben would agree with Dominic's comment about the past being the past, but it is obviously inextricably entwined with the future. There are still things I need to put right so that Ben understands what happened between us. He avoids that conversation; he says he doesn't care – let's just move on. It's as though he fears that if we look back it will overtake us again and everything will fall down around our heads. As though the past has to be smothered by this dazzling new future.

I fear that the Harringtons are the spectre of our future selves. Dominic and Susannah seem bored with everything in their lives, and with each other. Childless couples seem to live for each other, or else they just live for themselves. It feels like such an empty, pointless, unchanging life to me. It's children that create the seasons of a life: babyhood, childhood, adolescence and adulthood. Without them, Ben's and my life together will be static, unless we force some artificial change on it to keep ourselves busy.

It's hard to get past the idea that we are filling in time, making a life for ourselves other than the one we really wanted. A consolation prize when there is no consolation to be had. There is no point discussing this with Ben – picking it over is too painful for him. He's the pragmatic one. This is the blow that life has dealt us; we just have to deal with it. For him, the finality of the diagnosis was a gift. It was definitive, saving us years of hope and heartache. Now there is nothing to do but live with it.

After the warm days of autumn, November brings cooler weather and the house grows colder by the day. The evenings are a bit too cool to walk up to the village now. Instead we light the fire in the wood-burning stove in the kitchen and eat soups and pastas. We have gradually started inhabiting just a few rooms; the others are uncomfortably cold. Ben wants to leave the heating off until absolutely essential because of the cost.

Tonight it's really cold and we agree it's time to get some heating on. Ben opens up the radiators in our bedroom, one bathroom, his workroom and the summer room, where I've set up my work area on the long table. He goes down to the cellar to see how the boiler is handling it.

Every evening now, before I go to bed, I put on my coat and walk outside and close the front gates. It's partly security, not that we're at any risk in this quiet village, but more a sort of ritual to acknowledge the close of the day. To recognise this moment, not simply rush on to the next one. Outside the night is deep and quiet, a ghostly new moon suspended above the golden crown of the village radiant in the blackness. The air smells of fire and water and earth. When I stand out here in the velvety dark, there is the sense of timelessness. I can imagine this experience would have been the same a decade ago or even a century ago. My musings are interrupted by a distant pop and I turn back towards the house to find it in complete darkness.

Chapter Nine

The timing couldn't be worse from a work perspective and Ben is grateful when Dominic not only manages to get an electrician within days, but comes over himself to help sort the situation out.

The electrician, Monsieur Morel, is retired and so miraculously available, but clearly not keen at the same time. He doesn't speak a word of English but explains the problems to Dominic at length. Ben follows them around the house, up and down the stairs, and picks up a few words he doesn't like the sound of: in particular, *dangereux* and *mortel* – deadly.

Morel drinks the coffee Mia brings him while he scribbles down some figures with a stub of pencil on a scrap of paper he finds in his pocket. He adds these figures up, muttering under his breath, and finally hands the note to Dominic who raises his eyebrows and passes it on to Ben who feels himself go pale with shock.

He should have seen it coming. In a house this size everything is going to cost three times what it would for a normal-sized house. This expense will soak up nearly half of their entire budget. Playing the negotiator, Dominic enjoys a long debate with Morel and assures Ben that this is the outside cost. He personally guarantees it.

The bang in the basement marks the end of the golden days. The clear skies turn to pulpy grey clouds, the light flat and metallic. Cold seeps into the stone walls. Chill winds thread their way through every crevice as, for the next four days, Morel and his offsider, Enzo, tramp through the house. Their noisy drilling makes the whole house tremble, and all day they shout to each other up and down the stairs. Morel is well aware that Mia speaks French, but he will only discuss the job with Dominic, who arrives first thing in the morning and at the end of the day for updates. Morel apparently doesn't trust females with potentially deadly electrical information.

Dominic appears to be enjoying the experience but Ben is definitely not. He feels like a child having to wait for Dominic to come over and act as translator. He only managed three months of language lessons before he left Sydney and was sucked in by all the talk about immersion being the only way to learn. It's slow and frustrating. He might be immersed but he's also isolated. He has a collection of single words, nouns and verbs, but lacks the ability to join them together and has had to resort to a translator app, with limited success. The slightest deviation in pronunciation renders him unintelligible. Half the time he can't understand what people are saying to him or what he's even saying to them. It's made him realise how impatient he'd been in the past with migrants to Australia who didn't speak English. It seemed so basic. How would they possibly expect to make a life in an English-speaking country without the language?

Now he sees it's not that simple. It's a long, hard slog to proficiency, let alone fluency.

Mia doesn't care about the electricity being out. She's disillusioned with the twenty-first century and craves a quieter twentieth-century life. Ben manages to work things out with his scrum master and he and Mia find plenty to do around the house. By the end of the week they have power, heat and a very large bill to settle. But, as Dominic promised, it's no more than expected, which is something.

Chapter Ten

Dominic watches with detachment as Susannah berates him. He tries to recall when she developed this annoying habit of unnecessarily raising her voice. She used to be so calm and relaxed; so easygoing. Her voice was soft, even seductive on occasion. Now she screeches at him in a way that he finds embarrassing despite being the only witness. Has she actually become unhinged, teetering on the verge of some sort of breakdown – or is she acting? She's fairly convincing, so it's unlikely she's acting.

Now she rushes from the room and bangs around in the kitchen, the kettle whistles, the fridge opens and closes. Dominic puts another log on the fire and settles back with his magazine, anticipating the arrival of a nice cup of tea. But when she returns, calmer at least, it's apparently tea for one.

She settles purposefully into the armchair opposite him. 'I'm sorry I lost my temper, but . . .' She pauses, evidently tightening the rein on herself. 'I cannot understand why you would see it necessary to invite the Tinkers, as our guests, to one of the most expensive restaurants in the whole of Toulouse.'

Dominic has been thoroughly looking forward to this occasion, so it's disappointing that she's taking this adversarial position. Nevertheless, he's determined not to allow her to dampen his enthusiasm for the jaunt. 'Aren't we making them our new best friends? What better way to consolidate the relationship?'

'Dominic, it's not a business arrangement. We don't need to network with them. We don't have to impress them in the way you think. It is obscenely expensive and most likely not to the Tinkers' taste. *And we cannot afford it!*'

'Sus, you worry too much about money. Reggie won't mind —'

'Mind? I mind! I'm the one who has to call him begging for money. It's humiliating. Every time I call, I hear the disappointment in Daddy's voice.' She gives a little sob and comforts herself with a sip of her tea.

'That's your imagination, Susie. Reggie doesn't begrudge sending the odd feather for his little girl's nest.'

'I'm not a little girl and it's not the odd feather, it's a whole flock of . . . whatever . . . and it's every month! And there's no feathering involved! We need to pay the electricity bill so we don't get disconnected. A meal for four at Grégoire's would cost as much as that bill! You have to make an excuse . . . get out of it.'

'Oh, that would be awkward. A very poor show to invite, then un-invite.'

Her eyes bulge like a horse about to bolt. She tosses her head, completing the effect and it occurs to him it's probably menopause that makes her so mercurial; so easily frustrated.

'The Tinkers are real people, Dominic. They're not going to be dazzled by you swanning about lording it over everyone at

Grégoire's. Out-sommeliering the sommelier. They'll think it's pretentious. They will be embarrassed by you throwing money at them. Money *we don't have!*' She finishes with a shout, leaps up and gallops from the room, followed by the two mutts who loyally trot after her.

It's exhausting to watch Susannah expend so much energy agonising about money and lacerating herself at the prospect of having to ask Reggie to spot them a few quid now and then. It's coming her way eventually in any case, why not dip their fingers in now and pull out a few bob to make life more comfortable? It's not as though it will have any impact on Reggie, he owns half a mews in Kensington and collects rent from more than a dozen tenants. His coffers runneth over and they might as well flow to the needy.

Dear old Reggie. A typical Eastern European *émigré*, educated and cultured, who arrived with a battered suitcase, broken English and an over-developed sense of gratitude towards his adopted country. He started a small business buying and selling second-hand washing machines. Then new ones. Opened his own shop. Then another shop or five. Watches every penny and never had a welfare cheque in his life. Ninety years old and still the man about town, he's got a few good years in him yet. Dominic has grudging pride in his father-in-law, although he doubts very much if that's reciprocated – grudging or otherwise.

What Susannah fails to recognise is that Reggie *enjoys* playing benefactor to his youngest daughter. Her elder sister, Rebecca, has no need of assistance. She and her husband, the avaricious Simon, share Reggie's spartan philosophies. Those two have never known the joys of a gloriously decadent meal or glass of thirty-year-old Bordeaux. They famously won't even buy a bottle of water because it's available free from a tap. You can't get Evian from a tap. They prefer to channel their money into property and more property, and good on them, but there's more to life than wealth accumulation.

Dominic had relished the idea of taking their new friends to Grégoire's. The anticipation of the outing had him reminiscing about the old days when he had the time, money and friends to indulge in long lunches at London's finest establishments. Back then he had interesting and influential friends, none of your 'aspiring' this and that. One was an artist who regularly hung in the Hayward, another a music producer, a third was the managing director of one of Britain's largest newspapers, a fourth an ex-con turned bestselling author. Skilled raconteurs who kept each other enthralled from the first aperitif to the final brandy. People who shared an unspoken agreement that nothing kills the appetite like a bore. These were men with knowledge and opinions who were not afraid to voice them – none of your namby-pamby political correctness. He smiles, remembering how other patrons would often look longingly at their table, envying the hilarity and camaraderie. All men, obviously – few women can tell the simplest story without making it five times longer than necessary and dragging some emotional hoo-ha into it.

Yes, there was something luxuriant about a long lunch. Something decadent and self-indulgent that he has always adored, and the fact that all the other chumps were working was part of the pleasure. Back then he was also working. He'd never been one of those food critics who jotted in a tatty little notebook. He simply soaked it all up. The ambience or lack thereof, the demeanour of the staff, the professionalism of the serving process and then the main event, the food itself. He possessed the taste equivalent of a photographic memory: once tasted, never forgotten. And not just the flavour but the texture, fattiness, dryness, various aromas, both fleeting and volatile, consistency and the myriad flavours. His taste receptors had a workmanlike ability to deconstruct even the most complex dishes. He could discern which herbs and spices the chef had been heavy-handed with and identify even the most subtle of flavours. He could distinguish contrasts across an extensive continuum from sweet to tart. He could taste the quality of the butter, the oil, the salt and even the freshness of the flour. It was really endless and his virtuosity was utterly wasted on ninety-nine per cent of the meals served by establishments claiming to be restaurants. They were simply waiting rooms that happened to have (often substandard) kitchens attached. Those kitchens were staffed by the reluctant and the recalcitrant, motivated by the tyranny of the ticket machine and the threats of their superiors.

Grégoire's is a world away from all that. Chef Louis Lefevere has earned his two stars and continued to elevate his art. Not in an effort to grab that third accolade and satisfy some egotistical desideratum, but to continue dazzling and delighting his clientele. Lefevere is a softly spoken, thoughtful man and the atmosphere in the kitchen is one of quiet concentration. In short, Lefevere is Dominic's kind of chef, one who can be relied on for superior quality and immutable consistency.

Dominic is well aware that his tastebuds are not regenerating the way they once were; nevertheless they are still more abundant and vastly superior to most people's. This is partly a gift of DNA but mainly a lifetime of exercising them, challenging them and keeping them accountable. He regards himself as one of the world's elite, a person whose gift and vocation are perfectly compatible. The finesse of his palate is legendary. He'd been called a taste savant in his time, the Rain Man of gastronomy; this is his *raison d'être*. Naturally, Lefevere only knows him as Monsieur Harrington, the British expat with a refined appreciation for haute cuisine.

Dominic sighs, his pleasant reverie interrupted by the sounds of Susannah's distant sobbing. Hormones. Thank God to have been born a man. He could probably postpone the Tinkers' lunch for the moment; perhaps a windfall will come in the meantime.

Chapter Eleven

The village is shrouded in mist when Ben arrives to buy paint at the hardware shop, the French term for which is *la quincaillerie*. A tricky word he practised saying a dozen times but each time Mia corrected him. Frustratingly, he can't hear the difference between what she's saying and what he's repeating. They sound identical and he wonders if she's just being super picky.

He has arrived at *la quincaillerie* too early but decides to wait since there are limited opportunities to get through that door. It's closed on Wednesdays and weekends and not open until 10 a.m. on other days. Naturally, also closed for lunch from midday to sometime mid-afternoon. At home, hardware stores are guaranteed to be open for business twelve hours a day, seven days a week. Here retailing is more like a hobby. 'Yes, come by if you really need something. We'll probably be around' – indifferent shrug – 'just not too early, or at lunchtime . . .'

He leaves the car and walks up and down the street restlessly. There's nothing of interest in this part of the lower village. There is a café, which has little going for it apart from possibly being warm, but it isn't open for some reason. A dress shop with a window display that even to his inexpert eye looks thirty years out of date. The only attraction this morning is the smell of baking bread from the *boulangerie*. He buys a croissant and sits on a low wall outside to eat it.

The lifeless street and grey stone buildings are depressing. The cold here has a dull, heavy dampness to it. He looks to his phone for diversion and finds himself checking the surf-cam at Narrabeen where the glassy ocean mirrors the pale pink and aqua of the early evening sky. He watches a perfect set of five A-frames roll through, one after the other. A dozen or so guys, black specks drifting on their boards out the back, take it all for granted. The buttery croissant is cloying in his mouth, his body craves the sting of salt water. He longs for that clear dome of endless blue sky over Sydney and the smell of sunscreen baking on hot skin. He misses the drama of Sydney weather. The thick drowsy humidity and towering banks of cumulus clouds that signal the oncoming southerly buster; a cool change that belts through every house, slamming doors and windows, reviving the entire city from its stupor. Rain that comes down in such a deluge that you have to shout to be heard over it. That's what you call weather.

He feels an odd tightness in his chest, as though he might burst into tears. He puts his phone away quickly and looks up to see Thomas Van den Berg, the Dutch owner of the B&B, walking across the road and giving him a friendly wave. Although Ben finds him a bit annoying, he seems pleased to see Ben and asks how the house is coming along. He listens with interest to the story of the electrical problems.

'Of course. This is old houses for you,' says Thomas, always keen to make it clear that he has never been surprised by anything in his entire life. 'But you don't need to deal with Morel. He's a difficult character. There's a Brit here in the village who does all the expat work. Everyone uses him. Tony. Nice guy. Speaks the Queen's English. Mate.'

Despite Ben's efforts to explain to Thomas how to integrate the term 'mate' into a sentence, he persists in adding it as an awkward afterthought, like an exclamation mark.

'Dominic Harrington recommended Morel,' says Ben. 'Anyway, it's done now.'

Thomas shrugs. 'Two difficult characters. Members of a secret society?'

'I'm sure he had his reasons. Perhaps his pricing is better?' suggests Ben.

Thomas laughs out loud. 'The day a Frenchman makes a cheap price for a foreigner we can expect roses to fall from the sky.' He glances up expectantly, his palms open to the possibility. Ben's pretty sure that even Thomas would be surprised if it did happen. There's an awkward moment until he drops his hands with a disappointed shrug.

Ben forces a laugh. Who is the joke on here? Thomas going on about roses falling from the sky, or him for not being able to sort out these things for himself? It really is like being a child again; you only get told what people want you to know.

'Well, then,' says Thomas, sensing his little performance was less than amusing. 'Lana was going to get in touch and invite you for dinner. The business is quiet now. We'll close for a month at the end of December and go back home for Christmas. So, it's time to party.'

'Sure, great. I'll let Mia know. Actually, her mother's coming soon. You should come over and meet her. I'm just getting the paint for her room. She speaks Dutch.'

'Is my English not up to standard? Mate.' Thomas tilts his head to one side playfully. He laughs and gives Ben a friendly clap on the shoulder, saying they will leave it to the girls to set up. 'We will come to you and then you to us. As you know, Lana's an excellent cook. I hope you like herring – she does the best.'

Herring. Was there anything worse than raw pickled fish? Did that even qualify as cooking?

Back at the house, Ben lays out the drop sheets carefully and prepares the paint, stirring it thoroughly, dampening the roller and brush in preparation. He selects his favourite coding music, commonly known as psychedelic trance, puts in his earbuds and turns up the volume. Mia loathes this music, and he can completely understand why, but it helps him concentrate. As he rollers the white paint onto the old ceiling it glows like a strip of fluorescent light. He feels a sense of calm descend on him. This is the beauty of manual labour – your body does the work but your thoughts are your own. Programming is the opposite – the body is the demanding infrastructure that houses the workhorse.

Ben rarely lets his mind just wander. His thoughts are more regulated, like a committee meeting where issues can be raised and considered, decided or discarded. Mia and Olivia often bag him out about compartmentalising his thoughts – a male trait, apparently – as though this were a fault rather than an asset. It's his belief that the piling of one worry on top of another is what makes Mia get so anxious. Not just overthinking but intertwining everything in a big tangled knot where everything is dependent on everything else and there is no way forward and no way out.

One thing his work has taught him is that it's not a way to resolve problems. If there's a fault in the system, first isolate and identify the source and run tests to see which parts of the system are affected. Once the fault is accurately located, it can be relatively straightforward to resolve. That process can be applied to everything. Almost everything. Not love, for instance. When it came to Mia, he didn't seem to even have the ability to examine his choices. There's no compartment for her, she is the operating system and everything else is a peripheral. But as he works coating the ceiling, deleting the smoke and grime and everything that has happened in this room, the word 'folly' keeps coming back to him. He stops for a moment and checks it on his phone: 'lack of good sense; foolishness'.

Mia makes him foolish. He knows that. Buying this house had been the only way he could think of to get Mia back, to rescue their relationship. If it failed, it was on his head. They could both end up broke and alone. He had failed her once, he couldn't fail her again.

Chapter Twelve

Susannah lies on her bed crying furious tears, a pug tucked into each armpit. He calls it generosity. It's bloody well not. It's irresponsible. He's like a teenager who wrecks the family car and argues that the keys should never have been left around to tempt him. Reckless. Does she give him too much latitude? She shouldn't have to watch him like a child. What is wrong with him? It's pathetic the way he wants them to admire him. He couldn't admit the electrician had gone three hundred euro over budget, some stupid misunderstanding about the cost of materials. His French isn't as good as he makes out. He often gets things wrong. Could she confess to the Tinkers? Guilt-trip them into paying their own bloody electrician's bill? They obviously have plenty of money. They'd be so embarrassed. She couldn't bear it. After all, it's not their fault her husband is such an idiot. He'd have to make an arrangement with Monsieur Morel.

Lou and Chou snuggle closer and she strokes both their heads simultaneously and feels herself calming down. 'It's all right, my darlings. Mummy's just a little bit sad.'

On the other hand, she doesn't need Morel telling other people they can't pay their bills. The Atkins, for example. Or that ghastly Anne Hopkins. Everyone in the village talking about them. Gloating. She has no choice but to make the call.

Reggie answers the phone promptly enough but the conversation is unusually strained. He seems guarded. There's something she can't quite put a finger on. She's solicitous about his health and makes a point of asking after Mrs Hemming, his devoted housekeeper. He reminds her that today is Mrs Hemming's day off and he will dine at the club tonight, as he has every Friday for the last decade. He leads such a pleasant and untroubled existence, enjoying a delightfully cushy old age. Something she might have been able to experience had she not got caught up with Dominic all those years ago. Had she not become distracted from her career at a pivotal time. Had she not married a profligate who had no compunction about taking money from her elderly father. Nevertheless, she feels fortunate and grateful that Reggie is so indulgent. She knows he's not as generous with Rebecca who makes pots of money doing something in finance. Reggie is actually incapable of saying no; he can't bear the thought of his youngest daughter suffering in any way.

'Daddy, I'm so sorry, but I'm really terribly short this month, is there any chance . . .?'

No sympathetic tutting. No indulgent chuckle. Just a deep well of silence into which she finds herself tumbling. Something isn't right.

'Oh dear,' he says tonelessly, as though rehearsed. 'Becky hasn't spoken to you?'

'Becky? No, why? Has something happened?'

'Don't worry, my darling. Nothing terrible. We simply wanted to set things in motion for the future, for when I'm not around . . . I'm feeling a little weary these days . . .'

Tears push up in her throat. Is it the thought of Reggie no longer being there? Or panic at Becky's involvement in her financial future?

'. . . obviously Simon is in the investment game, so it made sense to give him and Becky power of attorney. They handle everything now. It takes the burden off me. I'm not on top of things the way I was. Now, even if I go completely gaga, your inheritance will be protected . . .'

Gaga? Weary? What on earth is he on about? He lives the life of a prince and has the constitution of a peasant. Was this plan his idea? Or has he been lobbied?

'Protected? From what?' she asks, even knowing the answer.

'. . . as Becky pointed out . . . quite rightly . . . better to do it now . . .'

His words are fragments of sound interrupting the whir of thoughts as she commutates this information. Becky and Simon now hold the keys to the kingdom? Her first impulse is to weep into the phone and beg her father for help. But even as that thought forms, as though anticipating it, he explains that they now pay all his bills and provide him pin money. He assures her that he is delighted with this arrangement. So simple and easy. His tone is gleeful. The king has found incorruptible guards to preserve his coffers of gold.

No point in challenging him. Deep breaths. Be sweet and congratulatory. Get off the phone before the tears come. Dry-eyed with fear, Susannah rushes from the living room into the kitchen to make tea. She stands staring blindly at the kettle as it comes to the boil. Lost in thought, she almost misses the sound of the phone ringing in the other room.

'Hello, darling, I hear you've spoken to Daddy. Sorry, dear, I didn't realise he hadn't kept you up to date with everything,' Rebecca says in honeyed tones.

'No, as a matter of fact . . . and I was surprised to hear . . .'

'Really? Perhaps it's a while since you spoke to him? It was all settled a few weeks ago. You know how generous Daddy is, giving money to anyone who asks. We don't want him eroding his capital, do we? I'm sure he's got another decade in him and by that time —'

'But am I able to get some sort of advance . . . we're just absolutely . . .'

'Darling, you've already had your advance. That was the house in Camden which you sold to buy the one in France —'

'We couldn't possibly have stayed there . . . you know that . . . with everything . . .'

'Plus the subsidies Daddy's provided you over the years – it's all documented.'

'They were gifts! You know they were.' Susannah struggles to restrain herself from shouting. 'I've had to mortgage the house. We only have Dominic's pension. No one could live on that.'

'People do, Susie. Many people. And they don't live in a beautiful house in France, either. They live in a two-up two-down in Hounslow, under the flight path.'

'You don't live in Hounslow . . .'

'I was just making the point that there are people worse off. Look, dear, I understand you have no understanding of how finance works. But clearly one member of the family cannot continue to draw down on their inheritance at the expense of a sibling. I'm sure you understand that.'

If only Rebecca's tone were less understanding and sympathetic, and achingly sweet. If only they were shouting at each other. Susannah's mounting panic makes her want to scream at someone, if only to find some relief.

'It's not your fault, darling. Daddy has made you dependent with his handouts. Too many fish and not enough teaching you to fish. Plus, of course, you married someone who is even less responsible than you are with money. You just need to curtail your spending and live within your means. Perhaps even sell the house and live on that. Or, you could consider getting jobs. I know it's a crazy idea, but that's what we do. We work.'

'But can't you even help me just this month? I'll never ask again. I had no notice —'

'I really am sorry but, truly, everything is locked away now. There's literally not a single penny floating around that I could spirit your way. You need to adjust to a new regime. Austerity measures, as they say. The full Greek.'

Susannah grips the receiver, almost paralysed with fear by her sister's obvious enjoyment of the situation. She has a sudden memory of Becky's wiry little fingers plucking at her flesh, pinching her arms and legs, urging her to cry, promising to stop only when the tears came. Threatening worse if she told. Whenever Becky caught sight of the dirty smudges she left behind, she would give Susannah a sly smile, her eyes bright with triumph.

'Good luck with it all, darling.'

'Becky, don't hang up . . . please . . . I don't know what to do.'

There is a long silence. It's difficult to tell whether Becky is pausing for further consideration or plans to drive the point home. Finally she says, 'I know it takes absolutely years to sell over there. You could rent the place out in the meantime and come back to London. And get a job. I have a little flat in Chiswick I could let you have cheaply until you get on your feet.'

'You know we can't come back! Why even suggest such a thing?'

'Well, *we* may not but I'm sure *you* could slip back into the country without any fuss. After all, you were, to some degree, an innocent bystander. That would rid you of your main liability in one fell swoop.'

'It always comes back to the fact that you hate Dominic,' says Susannah, vacillating between fury and despair.

'Susannah, when Daddy goes, you will get your inheritance. Not before. But I'll wager that within two years, you'll be broke again. Dominic worked his way through his mother's bequest, which I imagine was quite substantial, in a matter of a few years. Spent the lot on booze and grub, I'll wager. And he will fritter yours away as well. Daddy worked hard for years and years . . . do you really want to see all that go down your husband's gullet?'

Susannah fights the tears with everything she has left in reserve.

'And Susannah . . .'

'Yes?' Her voice breathless with hope.

'In case you're wondering, it wasn't our idea. It was Reggie's. He needed saving from himself.'

Susannah slams down the phone so hard it bounces off the hook and lies on the table emitting warning peeps.

Chapter Thirteen

Drifting clouds pattern the undulating landscape in varying shades of green as Dominic drives the winding road to Albi. Having broken the news to Susannah that they would be subsidising the Tinkers' electrical work, and having endured the histrionics that inevitably followed, he has set off to Albi to purchase some new shoes.

His thoughts turn to Ben. It's hard not to be intrigued by that young man's enviable confidence in his ability to generate income. At this stage, it's impossible to know whether that is the misplaced optimism of youth, or the reality of life on the *inter*net. 'Location independent', Ben calls it. For Dominic, acquiring money had once been relatively easy and painless. Now it's practically impossible. Both he and Susannah are unemployable. In fact, Susannah became unemployable without ever passing through an employable phase. But the Tinkers obviously have something going on that provides that surety of income.

While he has no plans to embrace technology at this late stage, there are times when Dominic has felt a smart phone would come in handy. Convenient, no doubt, to have the font of all knowledge in your pocket, although he finds it irritating the way people are so eager to whip it out and flaunt their search skills – which simply involves typing with their thumbs (quite a feat in itself), as far as he can gather. The problem is that learned people, with actual knowledge and expertise, are now considered bores. Make an attempt to promote intelligent discourse and you risk being branded a ranter. More admired is the ability to flit from one topic to the next, alighting briefly before moving on. It destroys any semblance of dinner-party debate and makes him grind his teeth to see people's heads suddenly bob down as they start checking things on their phones. What is the provenance of this information, anyway? Where is it coming from? They never seem to question that. Perhaps it all comes from the same source. The Wizard of Oz. It's like a religion – devotees with blind faith in this invisible world. Fortunately the Harringtons are no longer invited to dinner parties and so spared having to witness this dispiriting modern habit.

One of the most refreshing aspects of the Tinkers is that they seem to view modern technology as a tool, not a love match. They never wander around with their heads bowed, staring at their phones or substantiate information by saying they have seen it on Facebook or YouTube. Mia can be a struggle to converse with: there's something ephemeral about her, as though she's transiting through this world on her way to another. Perhaps he intimidates her. It's a maddening characteristic of the female of the species, their propensity for being intimidated. They have a preference for people who are 'nice'; anything stronger than neutral is considered intimidating. Susannah's forever gasping on about how *nice* someone is when in reality they are unbearably tedious. Mia isn't quite tedious but takes herself too seriously and so the potential is definitely there. Thinks of herself as some sort of artiste, no doubt.

Ben is more interesting. Intelligent and inquisitive about everything on a large and a small scale. The prospect of off-spring has never appealed to Dominic. Not for him the squalling baby, sticky-fingered toddler, disobedient child and surly teen-ager. Parents suffer through all that only to be cast aside and neglected once the children are no longer in need of a parent's ministrations. To happen upon your descendants as reasonable, independent, fully formed adults would be ideal. And Dominic would put his name down for a son like Ben, someone a father could be genuinely proud of. Although, had he and Susannah had children, then perhaps they could impose upon them now for funds or, as a last resort, a roof over their heads. It would be comforting to have a safety net to replace Reggie, who is a perpetual flight risk. The only thing that would change their immediate situation for the better was if Reggie suffered a moment's inattention crossing Kensington High Street, coincid-ing with the approach of the 452 for Vauxhall. But Reggie is a careful man. He always looks both ways. So that's an unlikely scenario. Still, nobody lives forever . . .

His thoughts wander back to Ben and how much he likes the fellow. Perhaps it's his Australian-ness, but he lacks any sort of pretension, any guile at all. He's like a man from an earlier era in many ways. He seems to find almost any subject Dominic raises interesting. It's quite extraordinary how well the two men get on, given the thirty-odd years age gap. Of course, Ben is not yet aware of the extent of the intellectual wasteland around them and not ensnared by the petty concerns of other members of the local community – and doubtless he won't be particularly interested. He's a man who likes to talk about 'things', not gossip about the doings of others. All in all, he is the best company one can hope for out here.

Dominic parks the car and, after a spot of lunch, enjoys a relaxed afternoon wandering the pleasant streets of Albi. He visits one of the galleries to view a Larsson exhibition, a delightfully twee perspective of nineteenth-century Swedish bourgeoisie, and then wanders around the old town until he finds the exact loafers he's been after for some time.

All his pleasant pottering comes to an abrupt end when his card is refused at the counter. '*Encore, Madame,*' he urges the assistant. '*Encore.*'

She adopts a neutral expression and repeats the transaction but his card is once again declined and she hands it back to him, like the worthless piece of plastic it is. '*Je suis désolée, Monsieur, elle est refusée.*'

Only slightly concerned, Dominic gets out his second credit card with the same result. He remembers he has a chequebook in the car but the assistant calls Madame la Directrice, a hard-eyed woman in her fifties who insists they don't accept cheques. This is a flat-out lie – the French trust cheques more than cards. Just not his cheques. While Madame argues the point with him, the assistant discreetly moves the object of his desire from the counter and puts the box out of his reach, as though she thinks him likely to grab it and run – like a delinquent!

He leaves the shop in a fury and hunts everywhere for a public phone, surely they still exist?! Apparently not. Despite the humiliation of the declined card, he's forced to return to the shoe shop and insist on using their phone to call home – only to find the line engaged! He waits five minutes, wandering around the store, under the steely eye of Madame and the assistant, and tries again. His efforts to communicate with his wife should logically reinforce the fact that there is an error not of his making. So why does he sense inward smirking behind those expressionless facades? He doth protest too much? Bloody supercilious French.

On the trip home, his anger is tempered by the realisation that he has less than a quarter of a tank of petrol and useless credit cards. The entire experience, the wasted day, the loss of a pair of beautiful kid-leather loafers, quite reasonably priced at just under a hundred euros, is further compounded by a visit to the bank where he is informed that the credit cards are all over limit and until they are paid there will be no more credit.

Now he stands in his living room looking at the wretched phone deliberately left off the hook! He shouts for Susannah, only to be met by silence. The pugs are noticeable by their absence. They normally recline on a large green velvet cushion looking like fat little fungi sprouting from a forest floor. The cushion is empty, only their indentations in evidence. So she is either out walking them, which is never far, or they are locked in her fond embrace upstairs.

Her door is shut. She must have taken the phone off the hook to nap. It's not as though they are inundated with calls, for Christ's sake! Typical of her, sleeping the day away while he's completely frazzled and frustrated by her financial ineptitude.

Chapter Fourteen

I have been so looking forward to the arrival of my mother, Eva, to have her witness our new life and, if I'm honest, validate our decision to make this move. She knows what we've been through and how we ended up here. I wanted to view our house through her architect's eyes. I knew she'd immediately see a thousand things we haven't noticed. I wanted to share the village and the little ateliers, which I knew she would love. And I wanted her company. Although any company would be welcome now.

Most evenings, after dinner, Ben has to join a compulsory 'stand up' meeting with the team at the start of the Sydney work day. The project is on a thirty-day sprint, so he's been working into the night as well as during the day, only appearing occasionally to complain about the internet speed. I've spent my evenings sitting in bed, where it's warm and comfy, binge-watching series on my laptop, which is probably what's slowing our internet, now I think of it.

This evening, while Ben goes upstairs after dinner, Eva and I stay at the kitchen table finishing off the wine and cheese.

'You need to make more friends,' says Eva, cutting off a sliver of roquefort and pushing the board away from her. 'Take that cheese away from me, please!'

'You can use your self-restraint, Mum,' I suggest with a smile, quoting one of her favourite lines. 'I know we do. It's a bit difficult right now with winter and Ben working all hours. You saw the village today, it's really quiet. There must be a lot of people who only live here in the summer. Even when we arrived in September there were loads of people around.'

'I just know it's going to get you down being on your own too much. You'll start thinking . . .'

Wrapping up the cheeses, I pour the last of the wine into her glass. 'And we know where that gets us, don't we?'

'I'm not entirely anti-thinking, it's just you need to keep yourself busy. Not become too introspective.'

'I know. We have these English friends I told you about, the Harringtons, and the Van den Bergs – you'll like them.'

'I won't like the Harringtons?'

'Susannah's nice . . . I'm not sure about him. He's a bit of a character. He's besotted with Ben. Treats him like his long-lost son. He's not that fond of me. He's one of those crusty old sorts who's not interested in anything women have to say and there's lots of topics that I wouldn't raise with him. Politics. Refugees. Feminism. Cheese. But that's okay. It's good for Ben; it's not easy for him here.'

'It's not easy for either of you. It's all very well speaking the language, but if you have no one to talk to . . . you're not in touch with the other guy, are you?'

'No, Mum. I'm not. As if. That's over and I wouldn't do that to Ben. He's made a massive effort to make things work for us. I'm not going to sabotage it.'

'I wasn't suggesting sabotage. That's not what I meant at all. I just thought if you were lonely . . . you might . . . that was part of the problem, I think. And also the other business.'

Twenty-four hours and she's already starting to get on my nerves. I get up from the table and stack the dishes in the sink. 'Mum, you don't need to find mitigating circumstances for me. And if we have to talk about it – which we don't – you can just say it. You don't need to call it "the other business" – it makes it seem worse. Like some sort of criminal activity.'

'No, we don't need to talk about it, but I don't want you stewing, either.'

'I have the right to stew if I want to.'

'Mia, darling, leave those dishes, I'll do them. Just sit down.'

I sit down reluctantly at the table. I don't want to talk about this right now. It still feels as though there is a dam of grief inside me that has set hard and just won't crack. My eyes burn with unshed tears. 'I actually feel like a complete idiot . . .'

'Don't be so hard on yourself, darling.'

'No, don't try to make things right – if you want me to talk about it, then listen to me! All those years Ben and I were living together and perfectly happy. Then the perfect, wonderful, amazing wedding. Exactly as I wanted it. When I think about all the energy and work I put into the styling and the place names and those stupid heart-shaped wreaths I made. The ridiculous things I thought were important. I'm so embarrassed by how . . . superficial I was.'

The pain in my mother's face sparks my tears. 'I actually *told* people we were getting married to start a family . . . like I was going to order online for immediate delivery. *One of each, please.* How stupid was I? I never thought . . . It was just so incredibly disappointing to find out in the end that it wasn't going to be possible. It was *never* possible! My body kept this secret from me all those years. It's completely broken my heart.' I pick up a tea towel and wipe my tears away roughly. 'That's why I wanted to come here. Partly for me and Ben and partly to get away from our friends and all the people who feel sorry for us. Practically all our friends have children now . . .'

'You're quite sure you don't want to look at . . .'

'I've told you before, adoption is incredibly difficult now. It takes years, and I just don't have the energy for more disappointment.'

Eva takes my hand and presses it to her cheek. 'I wish I could take this pain away. I wish I could suffer it for you. You have so much more to offer than that . . .'

'Don't tell me there are other things in life. Or I'll smother you with this tea towel.'

'I'll risk it.' Eva smiles sadly. 'Of course there are; you've got this wonderful project right here. It has so much potential. It's just calling out for your creative talents; for you to make your own mark on it.'

'I don't have a mark! I don't know what my mark even is! I feel as though being "creative" is just a childish thing you do, pottering around making things until you do something real and grown-up – and become a parent.'

'Children are a phase of your life, for a short time you're the centre of their universe, next thing you know they've gone to live on the other side of the world. The drive to create can apply to anything and everything, it can sustain you through your whole life. Actually, it was my job that got me through motherhood. I'm not sure I would have survived without that to nourish my soul and lift me out of the drudgery. Cooking, washing, driving – it felt endless. The creative urge will come back for you, I promise. You'll see something, a shape or a colour, and feel that urge to make something . . .'

'I pictured myself doing craft with . . . having a craft room . . . teaching them how to paint, and draw and sculpt instead of watching TV. I imagined what a great mother I would be. Taking them to exhibitions, like you took us. I still can't believe it was all just a fantasy. It seemed so real to me.'

'Darling, even if you'd had children, you'd find that picture was a fantasy. One minute they're creating a beautiful collage, next thing they're gluing each other's hair to it and inhaling the glitter.'

I can't help laughing. 'I didn't start that, by the way. That was Jonathan.'

'As usual. It's easy to idealise being a parent. It has its own set of hardships.'

I fold the tea towel in half and then quarters, storing it away neatly for future upsets. 'I didn't tell you but when we got the keys from the *notaire*, he told us that it had been in Madame Levant's will that the property should be sold to a young couple.'

'Seems an odd condition; it could have taken years for a young couple to come along.'

'Mum, she's dead. She's not keeping to a time frame.'

'You think she wanted children in the house?'

I nod miserably. 'I feel as though we've slipped in under false pretences. You saw that child's room, left there all set up.'

'What? You imagine it was left for you?'

'I don't know what to think. She was ancient, she can't have had a small child.'

'There are any number of explanations, it could have been her own room —'

'I thought of that. But it feels . . . I can feel a child's energy in that room. I've been having dreams about a child . . . a little girl . . .'

She gives me a long look. 'You have every right to be here, Mia. This house is yours now. You can fill it with whatever you want. Get out your pencils and paper, your brushes and paints . . . make a place for yourself here.'

'I've tried. It's not that easy.' I hate these angry, desperate tears that just keep rising up in me. 'Mum, I'm so scared that I'm never going to get over this.'

I can see from her expression she feels the same.

Chapter Fifteen

Ben likes Eva, he always has done. She's made it clear that she believes he's good for Mia. He likes Joe, Mia's father, but he's one of those friendly, preoccupied types who never quite connects. Eva's the plugged-in one; she says what she thinks but she's kind and generous too. Mia's two brothers are good guys but both intense. Mia's more the thoughtful, peaceful one; she's inherited Eva's gift for observation and shares her fascination with line and colour, textures and details.

As far as Ben's concerned, Mia's family are his family. His own family broke apart when his dad died. A death so unexpected, so sudden, that it took Ben years to process. It was years before he would even search the term 'aneurysm' online to discover the culprit.

The farm had been the central point of their lives – everything revolved around that. It was their home, their past and their future. His dad had been at the helm and, without him, everything solid and predictable simply dissolved. His mother sold the farm, paid off the debts and rented a little house

in town. The farmhouse had been old and generously propor-
tioned in the way the yellow villa is, designed by an architect
for wealthy clients. It had wide verandahs, high ceilings and
solid timber floors. The rented house was built for workers; the
rooms were small and dark, with lopsided additions attached
to the rear. Ben couldn't decide if his mother was now poor or
didn't care where they lived. Later, it seemed that she knew it
was going to be a temporary move. It was just for show. The
family had barely unpacked when Bradley Price, a neighbour-
ing farmer, began to show up. Coming home from school,
Ben would sometimes see him driving off in the afternoons.
His sister Olivia had her suspicions about Bradley. 'It's pretty
odd how he and Mum hooked up so quickly, don't you think?
Dad never liked him, you know.' Ben didn't want to think about
it but their mutual dislike of Bradley brought Olivia and him
closer together.

When the six-month lease on the house ended, his mother
announced that they would all be moving to Bradley's farm. He
was to become their step-father. Olivia was seventeen and still
believed she had some say in the matter. The next weeks were a
furious blur of shouting and tears and accusations. Ben had just
turned fifteen. He didn't consciously think about his father – the
loss was a dull heartache that became a part of him. His only
relief was found in sleep and weed. Bradley was no substitute for
his dad. Not even close. Ben had his own reasons for disliking
the man.

Olivia left for Sydney the day after her final exam. Ben
divided the next three years between school and his bedroom.
Each time he left the house, he averted his gaze and tried never
to look across the paddocks towards their old house, its dignified

profile a memorial to his old life. To a time when he was a member of a family.

In the evenings, he would come out of his room to collect his dinner. He pretended to listen to Bradley's complaints about his attitude and appearance, and slipped back into the shadows, eating alone at his desk. His mother only cared about what Bradley thought. Occasionally she would make excuses for Ben, but soon gave up in the face of her husband's hostility. Ben hated the way they would stare at each other hungrily when they thought he wasn't looking and sometimes, in the night, he would hear his mother cry out. Either in ecstasy or pain he never knew – never wanted to know. It felt like they were waiting for him to go and leave them alone together.

Ben was rescued from the loneliness of his existence by the camaraderie of coding. Programming appealed to his sense of order and fascination with patterns. He found a kinship online that was missing in his real life. As soon as he finished school, he followed Olivia to Sydney. He slept on an inflatable mattress on the floor beside her bed. She introduced him to her friends as her 'nerdy stoner brother'. Keen to shake that descriptor, he found casual work with a landscaper, stopped smoking weed and dug it up instead. A week into university he knew vet science was not for him; it was something his father had wanted for him. It was his sister's housemate, Mia, who convinced him he didn't have to do it; that he could do something he loved and he fell in love with her.

Eva is the ideal person to have here right now. She's beyond excited about the many architectural details of the house that Ben hasn't picked up on because he'd been overwhelmed by the scale of the place. She's pointed out the ornate floral plaster cornices and the ceiling roses above the lights, decorative mouldings on the walls, little crests and emblems everywhere. She examines the brass doorhandles, tarnished black with age, and finds little stories in each. She wants to know the history, the name of the architect, the story of the family who lived here. Her enthusiasm is adding another dimension to the house.

Last night he'd come down to the kitchen to make coffee and heard Mia crying. He was relieved that Eva was there to say the right things to comfort her. Things he struggles to articulate. He wishes he was better at it. He too wants to take her pain away. It's only now that he recognises the magnitude of the changes they have brought upon themselves. And now he's working flat out, that's another change.

Yesterday Eva and Mia walked up the hill and explored the village, visiting Mia's favourite ateliers: the jeweller and her artist husband, the leather-crafter, the clockmaker, the chocolatier. This morning the smell of baking wafts up from the kitchen and he has a fleeting sense that the house could one day feel like a real home. Thinking of home, he makes a video call to Olivia, on the off-chance that she's at her computer. Her face pops onto his screen with a wide grin. 'Hey bro, s'up?'

'Seriously, Ollie, you sound like an old person trying to act young.'

'I am an old person, remember? Thirty-nine this year, next year oblivion,' she says. 'How are you, my serious young insect? How's la belle France? You're lucky to catch me, was just about to shut down and go to bed.'

'Things are okay, yeah, good, actually.' There were so many things he had wanted to talk to his sister about but now they don't seem that important. He worries that expressing his concerns will breathe life into them. 'Eva's here now.'

'Oh cool, give her my love. We're having Christmas with them, did she tell you? They've rented a big house up at Byron. Me and the kids are road-tripping it up there.'

Ben feels a pang of homesickness for the December rituals of heat and holidays. 'Yeah, she did mention that. So you're not going to Mum's?'

'Nope. Not after last time. I've decided that's it. He's so rude to the kids. I think Mum's got Stockholm syndrome. I don't know how she can bear him. So, Mia said you've been working hard?'

'Yeah, it's not too bad, actually. Same team and Lei-Mae is running the project, so that makes it easier; she's really good. So we've got money flowing in again. Mia's still trying to figure out what she wants to do, so that's . . . you know . . . okay.'

'Benny Boy, it's not going to happen that you move to France and everything is magically perfect. Have you heard of the five stages of grief? Denial, anger, something, something, depression and acceptance. Oh, that's six . . . anyway, I think she's somewhere between the last two.'

'I don't know about that. It's more like she's incredibly disappointed that things are not going to be the way she thought.'

'And you are too, aren't you?'

'Obviously,' he says. 'Who wouldn't be? But there's no choice apart from accepting it.'

'Be patient. It's going to take time. It was a huge gamble going there but sometimes gambles pay off. If all else fails, I'll send the monsters out there for a month and you'll be put off children for life.'

'How are they? Mia told me Zach tried out for the school band.'

'Yep, he got into the performance band, so he's pretty happy with that. Still torture to get him to practice. I'm going to book him into surf school in Byron. Hey, Poppy's doing flamenco now – looks so cute stamping around in her little frilly dress. I'll send you a pic. I can't really afford all these lessons, work's been a bit slow – everyone's a bloody graphic designer these days.'

'You should be learning more code, there's front-end work around. I could put you forward on some projects.'

'Yeah, yeah, on the list,' says Olivia with a sigh. 'I can get Zach to teach me. Twelve-year-olds are ahead of the game now – he's doing computer science at school. Hey, let's catch up on Christmas Day and you can see the kids – our morning, after the gift opening.'

'Sure, I'll call you before then anyway. Good to see you, Ol.' Ben hears the note of sadness in his own voice. He watches his sister's face suddenly crease, her mouth pulled tight against the brimming tears in her eyes.

'Call anytime,' she says. 'Anytime at all. Love you, baby bro.'

'Yeah. Thanks, you too . . .' Her image snaps off the screen before he even finishes. He wishes he'd actually said he loved her instead of that half-hearted 'you too' that he always does. He loves her so fiercely it's hard to say out loud without the risk of bawling. He messages her that Zach's surf school and Poppy's dance fees can be Christmas presents from him and Mia and gets an exploding heart emoji in return. It makes him think about how the next generation of graphic interfaces might actually convey emotion.

Chapter Sixteen

On Sunday, in an effort to shake Susannah out of her torpor, Dominic suggests that they take an afternoon stroll and drop in on the Tinkers. It's cold, the sun pale and listless, reflecting the mood of his wife who has been in a complete funk for days, weeping over the money situation. Perhaps tiring of her own melodramatics, she reluctantly agrees and he chivvies her into a warm coat, even digging out her favourite angora beret and cheerfully looping a scarf around her neck. Enamoured with his own saintliness, he bestows a kiss on her forehead and pretends not to notice her flinch at his touch. You give your all, and this is what you get in return.

These days the walk is visually unrewarding; almost every tree is a grey skeleton. The fields, where bright-green barley, gold sunflowers and shimmering rows of corn grew in the spring and summer, now lie fallow. The soil, dark as coffee, furrowed and heaped in rows, offers an insect-rich smorgasbord for swooping birds. Susannah walks in silence, either lost in thought or continuing to sulk. Only the dogs in their ridiculous hooded tartan coats seem to be enjoying the outing.

There is no response to his knock on the Tinkers' front door, but he can see their car parked in the barn off to the side of the house. Susannah turns to leave, but since his involvement with the Tinkers' electrical problems, Dominic considers himself practically family with the usual familial rights of access. So, despite Susannah's protests, he has no qualms about venturing around to the back of the house to seek them out.

The Tinkers are in the back garden, but had he not been spotted, Dominic would have been tempted to slip away. He doesn't really know Mrs Van den Berg – Lana? – but is familiar with the husband, Thomas. They have grown sons, twins, whom they're always boasting about. Both boys apparently have civil service jobs in Brussels or The Hague or some other city blighted by bureaucrats.

Dominic dislikes Dutch people generally – the way they feel entitled to say whatever is on their minds with no attempt at diplomacy. They take a dim view of charm, seeing it as counterfeit currency. Thomas Van den Berg is no exception; he's combative and fancies himself as a wit to boot. The only thing in this couple's favour is that they do speak French and make an effort to involve themselves with the local community, not just throwing their hands in the air, declaring it all too hard and collapsing into the arms of the expat clique.

There's an older woman too, chatting away to Lana in Dutch. Initially he assumes the woman is a friend of the Van den Bergs, then notices her elf-like resemblance to Mia. Must be the mother elf. There are introductions all round. Predictably, Susannah is thrilled to meet Eva and treats the Van den Bergs like long-lost friends. It never ceases to irritate him the way she goes overboard in this regard. He knows for a fact that Thomas has offended Susannah on more than one occasion. At least her thespian training is being put to some use and Daddy's money wasn't completely wasted.

Thomas and Lana greet Dominic with polite detachment; Ben is more welcoming but it seems there is something a little reserved in his manner where before there had only been an openness. In any case, the moment passes and perhaps he imagined it. All the same, it does exacerbate his discomfort at finding the Van den Bergs making themselves at home with his new friends.

The women all appear very taken with each other, chatting volubly about nothing and everything, comparing notes, reinforcing each other's opinions the way women do. The four of them set off into the house together to prepare afternoon tea, leaving him with Ben and Thomas who begin to discuss internet speeds – was there ever a less interesting subject than this one? Although clearly fascinating to some people, given how often it's discussed nowadays. The *inter*net seems to make people obsess about the same things on high rotation. Ben actually invites Thomas to bring his laptop over and test it on their system. This seems all rather personal; isn't one's network something private – like a bank account? You'd hardly offer someone you barely knew the opportunity to pop some money through your account to test the efficiency of the service.

In a commendable effort to include Dominic, Ben explains the details of the software development project he's now working full-time on, one that will last three or four months but is broken down into what he calls 'sprints'. Thomas appears to have some understanding about Ben's work and asks seemingly intelligent questions – something Dominic would never risk – but Ben's responses are increasingly unintelligible.

'The other thing I've been doing, on the side . . .' says Ben, warming to his subject, 'is buying the source code for established apps, reconfiguring and adding new graphics and extra features, so upgrading essentially, and relaunching.'

'Ah, this is very cool. Is that completely legit?' asks Thomas.

'If you buy the source code, yeah. Once the app's up, it's set and forget. Plus you can make something from affiliations. You could make some real money if an app took off.'

Dominic understands all the words but at the same time has no idea what they mean. It's an odd experience, as if the language has been repurposed and now has hidden meanings.

He waits for the right moment to introduce a subject that he understands but then the conversation turns to something called cryptocurrency. The two younger men become quietly excited as they discover a mutual interest in blockchain, quantum computing and prime number theories. Ben is clearly the more knowledgeable of the two, with Thomas conceding that he's just getting a grasp on it. Dominic finds himself wearing the fixed smile of a simpleton, his gaze drawn towards the kitchen door as he waits to be rescued by the women. Finally, they appear with mugs of steaming tea and an uninspiring looking homemade cake. Whipped up by Eva, it is identified as a *boterkoek* – Dutch butter cake – and, despite its lacklustre appearance, proves a sweet salve to a tedious situation.

It seems that the Dutchies had just completed a tour of the house and Lana now raves about how wonderful it all is and how thrilled she is to see this old property being restored, behaving for all the world as though she were the local mayor with a benevolent interest in the wellbeing of her flock. Thomas reveals that, prior to the Tinkers' purchase, he came and viewed the house on their behalf, and it was he who lined up the utility providers ahead of time. So now the Van den Bergs seem to have developed a sense of ownership towards the property – and towards the Tinkers.

Perhaps sensing Dominic's discomfort, Ben takes him aside to show him a scythe he has discovered in the barn. Dominic picks up the tool, admiring the simplicity of the design. 'This revolutionised farming when it replaced the sickle, probably three hundred years ago,' he explains, relieved to resume his mantle of authority. 'It was a huge advancement on the sickle, which forced workers to bend and turned them into cripples. A very elegant solution.'

He gives it a few experimental sweeps only to be cautioned by Thomas. 'Be careful, we just sharpened it. It will slice your leg off without a second thought.'

As Dominic searches for an appropriate retort (one that's not entirely offensive) he accidentally swings the blade perilously close to his foot. Susannah gives a little shriek and Ben gently removes the tool from his grasp.

'Thomas was about to give us a demonstration,' says Ben.

Thomas takes the scythe in his hands and, with that infuriating smirk of his, explains: 'My grandfather taught me to use this tool when I was a teenager. Do you know, it's still actually more efficient than the petrol variety? It's a very beautiful instrument.'

Quite the showman, he swings into action. Rocking back and forth gracefully with swift and wide arching sweeps, he slices through the grass forming a long neat row to one side. Ben watches him with an expression of boyish delight. A smattering of applause from the ladies. Dominic helps himself to a second slice of *boterkoek*, apart from which the afternoon is clearly irredeemable.

Chapter Seventeen

Susannah has spent her morning following Dominic around the woods behind the house, picking up dead branches that he's noisily lopped off and cut up with a small chainsaw, something he's overly fond of wielding, always looking for an excuse. She's been enlisted to fill up sacks and carry them home. As a concession, to win approval and cater to the simpler tastes of their young friends, Dominic has invited the Tinkers and Eva over for pizzas to be cooked in the old bread oven. He had spent a couple of hours cleaning it out and now, as he and Susannah stack the wood neatly underneath it, he explains that he has some business to discuss with Ben, and she should therefore keep Mia and Eva busy preparing the pizzas upstairs, while the men tend to the preparation of the oven.

'I don't know why you have to do it tonight. You can talk to Ben anytime,' Susannah argues.

'Not alone and without interruption I can't.'

'Why don't you want anyone else to know? It's not something illegal, is it?'

'Of course not. O ye of little faith.'

'Is that really so surprising, Dominic? That I don't have faith in you any more?'

'Do you ever tire of hoeing that same patch of ground? Scratching away at the same barren plot to see if you can rake up something new? Susannah, everything that needs to be said on that subject has been said. You don't need to keep bringing it up.'

'Well, just don't give me something new to bring up!'

'I said a business idea, not a bank heist, for God's sake. I wish I'd never mentioned it.'

'Well, tell me about it. What is it?' Susannah hands him the last log with a savage thrust and begins to fold up the sacks.

Dominic heaves an exaggerated sigh. 'There's no point in explaining it to you, *ma chérie*. It's to do with the *inter*net. Besides, I'm not seeking your approval, just a modicum of cooperation. Is that really too much to ask?'

Susannah throws the sacks in the corner and stamps off upstairs. It's infuriating the way Dominic takes this superior stance on modern technology when he has no more idea than she does. He doesn't seem to realise how obvious his ignorance is, the way he enunciates *inter*net, *on*line and *e*mail, as if he alone knows the correct pronunciation of these terms. They are both marooned in the dark ages and no amount of poncy pronunciation can disguise that fact.

When the guests arrive, Susannah goes out of her way to be warm and welcoming. She's built a roaring fire in the living-room fireplace where they can gather for snacks and drinks. When the pizzas are done, they can just eat with their hands in front of the fire, super casual.

Eva seemed so lovely when they met on Sunday, but this evening she's almost too interested in the Harringtons. She glances around as though casing the joint or looking for evidence, peering into dark corners for something the Tinkers might have missed. Perhaps because they are younger, Mia and Ben refrain from asking personal questions. Eva doesn't follow any such protocol. She asks Susannah if they have children, where they lived in London, what plays Susannah has appeared in and why they left England to come to France. Susannah has been asked all of these questions before but not all at once. Expats don't tend to ask intrusive questions of each other; there's a respect for privacy and an understanding that some people may not want to share this information.

Distracted by this interrogation, Susannah hasn't noticed that Mia is sitting on Dominic's precious antique chair, until, returning with the drinks, he suddenly bellows, 'Not there! Sit anywhere but there!'

Mia leaps up, scarlet-faced, stammering apologies. Susannah feels herself flushing with embarrassment. For God's sake! The girl barely weighs an ounce; she's hardly going to break the blasted thing. Anyone would think she had taken an axe to it. Had Susannah noticed, she would have simply ignored the gaffe, suggesting Mia move to a more comfortable chair. Ben is clearly shocked, blinking with confusion, not knowing what crime has been committed. Eva looks horrified. Dominic barely apologises. Probably because he thinks his reaction was warranted. 'You couldn't possibly know, my dear,' he says loftily. 'Family heirloom. Seventeenth century, Jacobean. I won't say it's priceless . . .'

'Of course, it's not *priceless*,' interjects Susannah, guiding Mia over to the sofa. 'It's just a valuable antique. I'm terribly sorry he gave you such a fright.'

'Gave us all a fright, actually,' says Eva stonily. She gives Mia a look of maternal concern and in that moment, Susannah determines not to say another word on Dominic's behalf. She has spent twenty-five years defending him, explaining away his unpredictable behaviour, reinterpreting his comments, making him out to be eccentric rather than obnoxious. Even when he's been both drunk and obnoxious. From this day forth, his behaviour is his responsibility.

Unfazed by the upset he has created, Dominic launches his master plan, cheerily suggesting that Ben bring his drink downstairs and the men can attend to the oven. 'We'll let you know when it's at optimum temperature,' he says to Susannah, who pointedly ignores him.

When they've gone, the three women sit in silence until Susannah says, 'I'm so embarrassed . . . I don't know what to say . . . I'm really terribly sorry.'

'There's no reason why you should apologise, Susannah,' says Mia.

Eva agrees. 'Let's put it behind us. You have a lovely home, Susannah. Very comfortable.'

'Thank you, on both counts. So have you just come over to see Mia and Ben, or do you have other plans, Eva?'

'Mainly to help them settle in, but I'm also seeing family near Rotterdam next week.'

'Oh? Is that where you're from?' asks Susannah, relieved that the conversation is lightening up.

'No, I didn't even go to the Netherlands until I was in my twenties. I was born in Indonesia, and my parents migrated to Australia in the sixties when the Dutch were kicked out of the colony.'

'Mum speaks five languages,' says Mia, looking admiringly at her mother. 'Including Indonesian.'

Eva laughs. 'Not sure how good my Indonesian is these days. Most Dutch speak at least one if not two other languages. Actually, Mia's French is better than mine now. I need more practice.'

'So you'll be back home for Christmas?' asks Susannah.

'Yes, it will be odd without Mia and Ben, we usually have a big family Christmas . . .'

'Oh, but Mia and Ben must come to us for Christmas. Unlike the French, we'll celebrate on Christmas Day in traditional English style. We'd love to have you,' says Susannah. While Mia accepts the invitation gracefully, Susannah catches the doubtful expression on Eva's face.

Chapter Eighteen

Made of bricks, the bread oven is a cavity built deep into the wall of the alcove outside the cellar. Dominic had prepared and lit the fire a couple of hours earlier. Now he and Ben scrape out the hot embers with a hoe and wash out the floor of the oven, so that the pizzas will be able to sit directly on the bricks. While they wait for the temperature to cool to 350 degrees, the two men bask in its radiant warmth and drink their wine.

Dominic asks how Ben's work is progressing, hoping the response won't involve too much detail, but Ben seems disinclined to discuss his work as it's stressful right now. So Dominic has a free run straight into his business idea.

As he begins to outline his plan, even to his own ears, it sounds less like a plan and more like a collection of disconnected ideas with gaping holes that he had unwittingly anticipated Ben filling. He envisaged the younger man infused with enthusiasm at the prospect of working with someone of his stature, eager to bring his youthful skills and energy to the project. Dominic imagined them brainstorming together, mapping out ideas on paper, keen to meet up each day to push on with the project. He'd thought that perhaps they would form a company – Harrington Tinker Enterprises. Or the other way around if Ben was bothered by the hierarchy. Now he recognises Ben's expression as one of discomfort, his eyes clouded with doubt. Dominic hears himself rambling in a desperate bid to get traction.

Ben makes a polite show of considering his proposal but finally says, 'Look, this kind of business is not my area. I'm more involved in back-end architecture development. What you're talking about is more a marketing start-up. You just need a simple open-source content management system and a few plug-ins and you're in business. And I'm more than happy to show you how to do that yourself.'

Dominic waits expectantly, not sure if his idea has been dismissed out of hand. 'So, what do you think of the idea? Generally.'

'Look, I know you guys are not that tech-savvy and I'm no expert in micro start-ups, but what I can tell you in a general sense is that "experts", especially in the area of consumer reviews, are kind of "old school". The internet is a sort of democracy. It's a populist platform so it's hard to establish authority. With restaurant reviews, you can get a broader picture from a hundred – or a thousand – reviewers. With wine, you've got an insane amount of competition. It's all about algorithms these days. Plus it's near impossible to get people to pay for information when there's so much available for free. The only way you'd get it to pay its way is by subscription. That's a lot of work for probably not a lot of return – a long way down the track.'

So there it is. The great idea crushed and discarded in a matter of minutes. Dominic fights the urge to resist, to argue that amateurs couldn't hope to match his expertise and experience – let alone have the skill and wit to deliver an incisive review, whether it be to excoriate or endorse. A seasoned professional sets standards and holds an establishment to account in a way that a rabble can't hope to do. And who's to say complimentary reviews are objective and not simply the owner masquerading as a customer? Plus Ben is wrong about one thing: it's not democracy, it's anarchy. But it's pointless to argue. He'd asked for the boy's opinion and he got it. Now he feels like a fool. Worse, an old fool who's out of touch with the modern world. He has to regain his footing and not let Ben see his disappointment.

'Got it,' he says jauntily. 'Never mind. Back to the drawing board.' He tops up their glasses and raises his in a toast. 'To the drawing board. There's always another idea where that one came from.' But there isn't. There is nothing else to fall back on.

Ben checks the oven temperature again. 'We're pretty much good to go,' he says abruptly. 'I'll get the girls to bring the pizzas down.'

Dominic watches with envy as Ben takes the side stairs to the kitchen two at a time. He had a lot of energy at that age, although he didn't expend it on athletic endeavour but tireless debauchery. He'd fallen up stairs and down a flight or two. Clubs, bars, restaurants. Navigating your way inside was relatively easy, it was only on the outward journey that the perils revealed themselves. But no regrets. He'd do it all again, given half the chance. He had more excitement in those early years than these youngsters will have in a lifetime; they're wholesome as Quakers by comparison.

Unquestionably, Ben is a better man than he ever was. Ben is a worthy character. He's kind, caring and reliable, like a film hero. Nothing seems to faze him. He's primed for any eventuality and has a firm grip on the twenty-first century. He's part of the future world. He'd be an excellent business partner if that could be brought about. It's just finding the right idea. But that is a bigger discussion and not for this evening as he can now hear the womenfolk chattering as they bring the pizzas down. Mia is saying she loves corn on her pizza. Eva likes pineapple. The thought alone is distressing. Corn. But, there it is – sometimes you have to play along and act as though poor taste is acceptable because there is more at stake.

Chapter Nineteen

The afterglow of my mother's visit lasts for three days, then I start to fizzle. She's organised and systematic and, when it comes to renovation, she has an experienced eye for what needs doing and knows how to do it. She was sympathetic to our idea of not stripping wallpapers or discarding shabby furniture or trying to 'update' the place but working with everything that remains of the history, preserving it like a vintage piece. The three of us went from room to room compiling a master list of tasks in a foolscap exercise book she bought. 'One project at a time and complete it,' she told us. 'That way you won't get overwhelmed.'

I feel completely overwhelmed. When I was young, it took me years to learn how to tidy my room. I could never figure out how and where to start. Putting one foot in front of another just doesn't come naturally. I'm more a dancer than a plodder. Both my mother and Ben accept this failing in me, even if they find it hard to understand how something simple can be made difficult. When I start an art project, it's more like picking at the edges, teasing it out, seeing what could be. Once it's going somewhere, it's like falling in love – exhausting and exhilarating and you can't think of anything else. It's disorganised and chaotic, and I'm fine with that.

Eva began a project to get me started. We scoured out the downstairs bathroom and regrouted the wall tiles. It's not that I'm uninspired by the bathrooms, all four of them are amazing as far as bathrooms go. Each one is spacious and decorated with patterned and plain tiles in bright yellow and royal blue. The baths and pedestal basins are either soft yellow or pale blue. They've been cared for and are in good condition. That first bathroom is finished but, now my mother's gone, I can't seem to make myself start the next one.

I make excuses and procrastinate. Against my will, I find myself spending hours online looking at images of interiors of other people's houses. I think about all the things that *could* be done without having any motivation to do them. I worry that I'm becoming a spectator, preferring to dream about things rather than take action. There's no pleasure in being so lazy; it makes me feel guilty and miserable.

Ben doesn't say a thing about it. He's not one of those people with secret expectations that can never be lived up to. Perhaps it would be better if he was and I'd feel under some pressure. Now I'm making it his fault. The idea to buy this house was so unlike him, I felt it was my duty to come to the party. I'm just not sure how committed I really am.

At the time, we had been living apart for three months. Our separation wasn't dramatic – there were no angry scenes, just sad ones. It wasn't formalised or finalised, it was a kind of trial separation that didn't make either of us feel any better. We had withdrawn from each other in different ways and in opposite directions. Things that needed to be said were too painful to discuss. Right from the start, Ben couldn't seem to grasp the depth of my devastation. He never talked about his own feelings. That hasn't changed. I have to accept that he doesn't understand and will never understand. Perhaps my expectations weren't reasonable. There's no doubt he does his best. But it was that crack in our relationship that allowed Isaac to slip in between us.

I was happy in my teaching job. I didn't enjoy the admin or the growing obsession with assessments, but loved working with kids and their crazy imaginations and wild ideas. People lose that pure creativity later on, when ego and the need for recognition worm their way into the creative mind. I enjoyed teaching the kids how to express their ideas. I loved the noise and chaos of the art room. It was rewarding to see talented and hardworking students have their final-year work among the select few to be exhibited in a public gallery, the Art Gallery of New South Wales, no less.

When I discovered that I could never be a mother, it mysteriously soured my work for me. I wish it could have been otherwise. It wasn't conscious, it wasn't fair, it just happened. Over the next few months my work became exhausting, stressful and eventually debilitating. I felt gloomy and irritable. The students' high spirits grated on my nerves. Some days I couldn't bear to go to work and would call in sick. I was being eaten away by grief and the pointlessness of my life.

It was Eva who suggested I take a year off to try to get my mojo back, do something different. By that stage, I didn't really have a choice. Desperate to escape the misery that was crushing my soul, I convinced myself that change was the answer. I would change *everything* and begin again. It was as if I needed to blow up my life to find out what could survive the blast. Ben hid his devastation when I suggested we have a trial separation. He was kind, understanding and helpful. I didn't know what to make of that. He probably should have just stopped me. Talked me out of it. I wasn't quite right in the head. But that's not his way.

I moved into a share house with strangers and found a part-time job in an art supplies warehouse in the city. I've always loved art supplies. The textures of watercolour parchment under my fingers, the oily smoothness of a graphite 10B, the boxes of neatly aligned watercolours and acrylics, their names familiar from my earliest memories: cadmium yellow, red ochre, ultramarine blue, titanium white. We sold the raw materials of infinite possibilities for expression.

I missed my students, but I had nothing left to offer them. I missed Ben but I had nothing to offer him either.

Isaac bought his art supplies there. He was strikingly handsome, fine-featured with blue-green eyes and dark curls that made him look like an artist from an earlier century. He often stopped to chat with me about what he was working on and showed me images of his works in progress. He was talented and beautiful. In our conversations he revealed that he lived alone in a flat attached to his parents' house in Bellevue Hill. They were benefactors of the arts and supported his artistic aspirations. He invited me to the opening of an exhibition of his work in a small gallery in Rose Bay. I stepped out of my world and into his, and went home with him that night.

In the weeks that followed, I saw him more often than I really meant to. He was sweet and sensual and self-involved. He was like an intoxicant that distracted me from my torment. I was self-medicating by imagining myself to be in love with him.

But I knew already that we could never flow together the way Ben and I had all these years. I knew we had no future together.

In the end, I had to tell Ben. It was only fair. He came straight round to the house where I was living. We sat on the bed in my gloomy little bedroom. I had never seen him so upset, so furious and so absolutely convinced that this was not the way things were meant to be. He had thought he just needed to wait for me to come around. He was giving me space, he said. Now he realised that he'd let me drift too far and I'd drifted away.

'Mia, I'm here for you and I always will be and I'll do whatever it takes to fix what's broken between us,' he told me. He gave me a spreadsheet he'd been working on. It listed and cross-referenced everything he loved about me under the headings of *Attributes*, *Qualities*, *Abilities* and *Random*. He explained that it wasn't finished, it was a work in progress, but there were already twenty-six items ranging from my habit of getting hiccups from too much wine to the heart-shaped freckle on my shoulder to my ability to knit and sew. The spreadsheet of love. It came to me at a time when I found myself completely unlovable. It wasn't us who was broken, it was me.

The next time I heard from him, he messaged me a link to the *immobilier* in Cordes-sur-Ciel and the image of the yellow villa still for sale. I had lost myself and now this is where I find myself.

Today is bitterly cold, there's not one warm spot anywhere in the house and I head straight back to bed. At lunchtime, Ben brings sandwiches and tea upstairs. 'Aren't you feeling well?' he asks kindly, sitting down on the side of the bed.

'I'm good. Just . . . you know, hibernating. Waiting for the thaw.'

'Probably more comfortable here. The fire's gone out in the kitchen,' he says.

'Oh, sorry. I must have left it on too low . . . I can relight it.'

'We're out tonight anyway, so don't worry.'

'I'll get it going first thing, before you even open your eyes in the morning,' I promise, feeling like the worst kind of self-indulgent waster.

'Are you feeling down about Eva going? What were you saying to her about a child?'

'Were you two talking about me? The one I keep dreaming about, I've told you.'

He frowns. 'Who is she? I don't get it.'

'I feel as though something happened to that little girl. I need to find out —' I say, feeling suddenly breathless.

His expression goes blank and he says carefully, 'Mia, all sorts of things have happened in this house in the last hundred and fifty years. We don't need to find out about them. They have nothing to do with us.'

'I don't need to know everything. I only care about her. I have a sense of her here in the house . . .'

Ben looks so worried I immediately regret even mentioning it. 'It's okay, I just mean I'm curious about her. I don't mean she's haunting the place. Forget it.' I smile but he's obviously not convinced by my quick turnaround.

'Why don't we renovate that room, if it bothers you?'

'It doesn't bother me, but maybe it's a sign . . . maybe something could happen for us.'

Ben gets up and goes to the window. He stands there staring

out into the grey afternoon. 'I knew that was where this was going. Nothing is going to happen, Mia. And if you think it is, you're kidding yourself. Let it go.'

I know he's right but I can't seem to shake this feeling. It's impossible to describe: this child is not like a ghost or a spirit; there is more the sense that I am waiting for someone to come home.

When he goes back to work, I force myself out of bed and get dressed. I stand at the bedroom window, my hand pressed against the icy-cold pane. It's the middle of the afternoon and already twilight. All day the sky has been heavy with thick yellowish cloud; now tiny flecks of white spinning and floating like summer blossom gust past the window. I feel quite excited at the idea that this might be snow and wonder if the idea of snow and the reality of it will be another gap, another disappointment.

As I reach to pull the curtains closed, I notice a figure at the gate. In the dim light, it's difficult to make out any detail but I'm certain it's the woman with the brown hat again. She always seems to pause and look at the house in the same way, but with no intention of coming in. It's like she's checking on it, or on us.

In our new world among strangers Le Bleu de Pastel, the Van den Berg's B&B, has a comforting feel about it, like the home of old friends. We stayed there on our earlier trip and again when we first arrived. Now it's closed for winter, so we don't need to share the Van den Bergs with paying guests at the *table d'hôtes*. This will be our last get-together for a while, as from mid-December they always take a month off and go back to the Netherlands. Eva was right – we do need to make more friends.

Thomas and Lana are both great cooks. The Harringtons have a complicated intellectual relationship with food. Susannah is always so eager to please, keeping everyone happy but not really enjoying herself. And anyway, you get the idea that nothing is ever quite up to Dominic's standards. Lana and Thomas are more like us – they just enjoy food and there is a more relaxed sense of *bonhomie* at their table. Tonight they serve up a delicious rich cassoulet with baguette and a *vin rouge* from nearby Gaillac.

'I must apologise, Ben,' says Thomas, as we settle down to eat. 'We were right out of herring. I know you will be disappointed, but we'll make it up to you some other time. We can have three courses of only herring, herring soup, baked herring and, of course, herring soufflé – it's the best.'

'Book me in,' says Ben with a grin. 'We can return the favour with a barbecue of charred sausage and fatty chops.'

'Okay, let's call a truce on the cuisine wars,' says Lana. 'You're putting me off my meal.'

'On another topic, have you guys seen a woman who walks down our road almost every day? Older woman, wears a dark coat and brown hat?' I ask.

Lana considers this for a moment. 'Oh yes, I think I know who you mean. That's Madame Bellamy. She lives in one of the cottages further down from you.'

'Did she know Madame Levant? Was she a friend?'

'She used to work for her,' says Lana. 'You know Madame Levant was very old, somewhere in her nineties. I'm not sure what Madame Bellamy did exactly but I think she was like a housekeeper.'

'When we arrived, ten years ago, you would see Madame Levant about the village,' says Thomas. 'She was quite distinctive.'

'Oh yes, everyone knew her. Very elegant and stylish. In the last few years before she died, you didn't see her at all. I suppose she was unwell,' adds Lana.

'Do you know anything else about her?' I ask.

'Not really, I'm sure she must have had close friends here in Cordes. I believe she was born in this village,' says Lana. 'Someone said she lived in Paris for years. But that's all I know.'

'Levant's not the family name, though,' says Thomas.

'Ah, that's right, Levant was her married name. I think the family name was Dupont.'

'So she didn't have a family, or children?' I ask. 'Or grand-children?'

Lana shrugs. 'I don't really know.'

'Do you think there's any significance with the house being painted such a strong shade of yellow?' I ask. 'The only others I've seen are more ochre.'

'Do you mean because of Van Gogh's house?' asks Lana. 'I'm not sure that would have been the family's intention; I think that's something only artists would know about.'

'Or Dutch people,' adds Thomas. 'We make it our business to know everything other Dutch people do everywhere.'

'There's a "Yellow House" in Sydney. It was an artist's collective back in the fifties and sixties,' I tell them. 'So what's the origin of the name *Le Bleu de Pastel*? You have an affinity for the colour blue?'

'You haven't heard of *le pastel*? It's a plant that makes a deep-blue pigment – at one time there was a huge industry around it here. They called it "blue-gold" – very valuable,' says Lana.

Thomas consults his phone and reports: 'The English name is woad, *Isatis tinctoria*, to be precise. If that means anything to you.'

'That's right,' says Lana. 'In France, it only grows between Albi, Toulouse and Carcassonne. It made this whole area incredibly wealthy in the fifteenth and sixteenth centuries but then, as we know, all good things come to an end. Indigo from India was much cheaper and so the trade "dyed" out. That pale-blue scarf I sometimes wear – I wore it to your place last week – was hand-dyed with *le pastel*. If you're interested, I can introduce you to someone who works with the dyes.'

Thomas turns to Ben. 'Mate. I need to ask you. I deposited Ether into my cold wallet and I don't know why, but it took a while to come through.'

Ben's more than happy to switch to one of his favourite subjects. 'Different exchanges have different confirmation times. It should take the miners around thirty confirmations to process because it goes through the ECDSA on the blockchain to keep the ledger. But, you know the higher the gas limit, the quicker the transactions, right?'

Lana turns to me and says in French, 'Ignore them. We have our own secret language.' She speaks excellent French and right now she's the only person I can have a real conversation with outside my day-to-day transactions. It's become a bit of a sticking point with Ben, but I adore speaking French, and love the chance to stretch myself with an in-depth discussion. So, while the men wrestle with the intricacies of cryptocurrency, Lana and I talk about colour and natural dyes using vegetables and leaves. Her passion is ancient history and she knows all about mordants and old methods of dyeing wool and fabric. She suggests that, when they return from holidays, we go foraging in the woods and do some experimenting. For the first time in a long while I feel that tingle of interest that I can't quite put a name to.

Both our conversations make me realise how much more we have in common with Lana and Thomas, who are closer in age to us. We inhabit the same world, whereas the Harringtons seem to live in an earlier time – and on a different planet.

'So, how are you getting on with Monsieur Harrington?' asks Thomas, reading my thoughts.

'He's a funny one,' says Ben affectionately. 'He's not a bad bloke.'

Lana looks at me. I'm not going to lie to agree with Ben. 'I don't find him funny. He's unbelievably rude.'

'Oh brother, the chair again. Look, that was a one-off incident,' protests Ben.

'He's got this "special" chair, right? I thought it was just a chair for sitting on, like other chairs. I sat on it for about five seconds and he *yelled* at me to get off it.'

'What? Oh no, that's terrible . . .' Lana looks at Thomas as though he might have an explanation.

Thomas shrugs philosophically. 'He's his own man, as they say. He has a strange sense of humour, normal rules don't apply —'

'That's how I see him too,' says Ben. 'He's just a bit different. He's a really clever guy.'

'You're making him sound interesting and eccentric,' says Lana. 'He's not!'

I agree with her. 'He might be clever but I think men would have a completely different impression of him. He has absolutely zero interest in anything I have to say. Old-school misogynist.'

'Wow, that's harsh.' Ben seems surprised I feel so strongly.

'I agree one hundred per cent! He ignores me and he didn't like seeing us at your house last week. He was quite annoyed,' says Lana. 'He wants you all to himself.'

'Well, let's not fully attack him.' Ben hates talking about people behind their backs.

'No, let's not,' says Thomas. 'I will say one last thing on this subject. I am curious to know his secret.'

'What do you mean?' asks Lana.

'Well, you know, many people come to France to reinvent themselves. They start a new story where no one knows their history. I'm sure of two things. Number one, that the "Harringtons" have an interesting history and, number two, that their name is not really Harrington.'

'You've never told me this!' says Lana. 'How do you know?'

'That's because I'm not a gossip but a man of great discretion. I happen to know that they don't have mail delivered, they collect it from La Poste and I have noticed that it's not addressed to Harrington. I couldn't quite read the name . . . but, it's short, I would say four or five letters at the most.'

Lana gives a huff of disapproval. 'This is too much, you're looking over his shoulder now?'

'Worse than that,' admits Thomas without remorse. 'Susannah was supposed to be a "well-known" actress but on the internet she doesn't exist anywhere. Neither of them do.'

I laugh. 'So you've been stalking them! She might be under her maiden name, or . . . wasn't she married before?'

Ben is shaking his head in disbelief. Lana agrees. 'No, this is going too far. I think we should leave it and forget we had this conversation. It's not nice. It's not friendly.'

Thomas shrugs. 'So there it is. Ask me no more questions. We will leave the matter there and prepare ourselves for a delicious *appeltaart*. Mates.'

Chapter Twenty

Having now applied every possible austerity measure, Susannah is exhausted from sleepless nights and constant fretting. Apart from the phone in her room, all extensions have been unplugged to prevent Dominic making overseas calls. The heating is turned off and, sooner or later, the power will be disconnected, the phone cut off and the bank will call in the loan. She has run out of ideas and lacks the energy to implement them anyway. She sits in her room all day long, tucked up with the dogs, watching her favourite DVDs: *Casablanca, Rear Window, Sunset Boulevard*. She must have watched *Blow-Up* a dozen times. It's as though she has been diagnosed with a terminal illness and now fills her last days with nostalgia and old pleasures. Actually, something terminal, preferably dignified and painless, wouldn't be so bad – at least there would be an end in sight to this misery. The knowledge that her days are numbered might reawaken her to the beauty of the world. If she had a terminal disease, she would not be spending her last days here.

Occasionally she gets up to let the dogs out and wanders the house like an invalid, dressed in her woollen dressing-gown and slippers. Dominic has been locked in his study working on his new money-making scheme: his memoirs. Obviously Ben didn't think much of his previous idea – whatever that was – since it's been jettisoned. Now he talks grandly of agents and publishing deals, speculating on the inevitability of a bidding war. She dreads to think what he's putting in it. He has the ability to shovel fiction on to the page and tweezer in the tiniest details to make it believable. What tales is he spinning about the past – and especially about her? How will he whitewash himself and justify his despicable behaviour? The press will tear him to shreds. But what can she do, given he seems determined to hang himself out to dry? It's not just for money – he craves the attention, not seeming to concern himself about whether it's good or bad. Hopefully it won't get published at all. And if it does, she can only pray that it ends up in a discount bin before anyone reads it.

Susannah will not be reading it; she has no desire to revisit her history with Dominic. The infamous 'good times' are long forgotten and she wonders how much pleasure she really derived from them. Dominic remembers the detail of virtually every decent meal he ever ate, every bottle of expensive wine he consumed and every celebrity he met – regardless of how inebriated he was at the time. She remembers none of that. She does remember the time before Dominic.

Through the rosy prism of nostalgia, her marriage to Maxwell now appears as a sanctuary, a tropical island where the sun always shone. Unfortunately tropical islands become boring. A quiet affair with another actor might have taken the edge off it for her. Maxwell probably could have borne that, had she been discreet. Ten years her senior, he was the more mature one and faithful to her partly because he wasn't particularly interested in sex, let alone conquests. Initially she worried that he was gay but later realised that he simply wasn't driven in that department. He would oblige her and was a tender, considerate lover, but he was besotted with nothing in the world so much as his work. *That* he adored, rejoicing in every aspect of it.

In the long run, Max's love affair with the theatre had served him better than any relationship could. Two decades later, he is still working, having enjoyed a string of successes on both sides of the Atlantic. It's devastating to realise that with a little restraint, or at the very least, discretion, she could have been enjoying the fruits of his labours. These days he has an apartment in the Upper West Side, a house in Chelsea and a villa on Capri where he entertains celebrities and patrons of the arts in the summer months. All this thrown away as a result of her impulsive, capricious nature.

Maxwell had been endlessly kind. It wasn't just that she was bored – she wasn't entirely superficial – but those years in her early thirties had been difficult. Career prospects were already withering, roles being snatched up by younger and more talented actresses. Her social life was frenetic, but everyone seemed brighter, wittier and more ambitious than her. She wasn't really sure who she was back then. Dominic saw a version of her that she found appealing. He was the polar opposite of Maxwell. Although he was sometimes cruel, ridiculing her ideas, flirting with her friends and making her the butt of his humour, he was impulsively romantic. There were passionate love notes, gorgeous bouquets of roses, feverish afternoons in grand hotel rooms.

He adored sex and was insatiable in that regard. If Maxwell had made her feel less than desirable, Dominic made her feel irresistible. And she didn't resist. The fact that Dominic had a wife somehow escaped their attention. Until his wife found out. Then it came to everyone's attention. Cars were coined. Windows smashed. Michelle hectored Maxwell, who may have taken a more measured approach, left to his own devices. Determined to create maximum embarrassment, Michelle contacted all the tabloids and told the story of the director, the critic, the actress and the wronged wife. The papers, as they say, had a field day. It was only later, realising Michelle was pregnant at the time, that Susannah could understand the scale of her reaction. Dominic had been desperate to keep the combination of his face and his profession out of the press. Every photograph showed him shielding his face with anything that came to hand. Within a day or two, the press had tired of the story, but both marriages were over.

Susannah and Dominic settled down together among the ruins; both had fared badly financially. No one in theatre dared cast Susannah but she got some small roles in films as a result of the exposure. Dominic funnelled his bitterness into incisive reviews, decimating several bistros whose food had obviously offended many readers because his column became more popular than ever and he was poached by a rival publication offering more money. The divorces had been exhausting for both of them and, to some extent, their interest in each other had waned. It seemed that half the attraction had been the covert nature of their trysts. Secrecy, intrigue and paucity had fuelled desire but once they were living together the law of diminishing return came into play. They had to adjust to each other, to compromise.

In the end, Susannah felt they got married to prove something. It's very difficult now to remember exactly what that was.

So much time has passed since her last acting role, but perhaps she has reached an age when she might be considered for character roles. Lady Macbeth? These days she could do madness quite convincingly. She tries out a couple of half-remembered lines and sounds every bit as broken as a woman who has ordered the murders of innocent people. Her voice has taken on a different quality, her suffering evident in its timbre.

She picks up the phone, longing to hear Maxwell's voice – even his voicemail would be comforting – and is surprised when he answers straight away. 'Max? Darling, it's Susie,' she says in a hushed voice.

'Susie? You'll have to speak up, I can hardly hear you.'

She slides down in the bed and pulls the covers over her head. 'Is that better?'

'Ah, much clearer. To what do I owe the pleasure?'

'Oh Max, don't be like that. I just wondered how you were.'

'You know I don't have a cynical bone in my body, but you rarely call me to find out the state of my health. Anyway, I'm busy as usual. Two new shows opening in the new year.'

'I haven't been to the theatre for so long . . .'

'Let me know next time you're in town. I'll get you a ticket and we can meet for supper.'

'I'd love to. I would love that, Max. I was wondering, do you think there would be any new opportunities for me, parts in . . . older . . . character roles . . . I mean, older women are all the rage now. Look at Helen Mirren.' There is a long silence on the other end and she adds quickly, 'I'm not . . .'

'Helen Mirren has spent her life becoming "Helen Mirren". You haven't really kept your hand in, have you, my dear?'

'I know, I didn't mean . . . I'm not comparing . . .'

'Does this mean you're coming back to London?'

'I'm considering my options. Rebecca has offered me a flat . . .'

'I still see Becky and Simon from time to time – they're keen theatre-goers, as you know. So, I'm aware of your situation.'

'It's bad enough having a "situation" without all the world knowing about it,' says Susannah.

'I'm hardly all the world, am I? Becky is obviously concerned about you.'

'I don't know what to do, Max. I don't know what to do . . . tell me what to do.'

'Your acting skills may be a little rusty but that can be worked on. Some things are timeless, and you have a dignity – a natural gravitas – that will only be enhanced by maturity. I just wish you'd stuck with it when you were younger – you could be a Helen Mirren now. Anyway, we're only a couple of weeks out from Christmas, so there's nothing happening now. But I do have something casting in late January; there might be a walk-on for you . . . I can't promise anything, but let's be in touch after Christmas.'

Susannah is tearful with gratitude. 'Anything, anything . . . I would be so grateful . . .'

'Chin up. Enjoy Christmas. It may be your last in exile.'

Susannah feels a warm surge of relief. Life is looking up. She gets out of bed and dresses quickly. She catches sight of herself in the mirror, her unconscious self, without make-up, hair tied back, body encased in thick winter clothes. For a moment she glimpses something else: the beauty of age, perhaps even a touch of gravitas.

Cheered, she lets the dogs out, makes tea and takes it outside to sit in her arbour in the watery sunshine while she tries to marshal her thoughts. She will take the dogs for a walk later and collect some firewood on the way. This evening she will cook something decent instead of cobbling bits and pieces together. She feels uplifted by a sense of hope she hasn't experienced in months. Maxwell will look after her, she can depend on him.

She looks around her, thinking how much she loves the shelter of the arbour and being surrounded by glorious roses in spring and summer – it's like a secret place you have as a child. The brambles are bare now; they need a good hard prune. The thought brings a creeping sense of uncertainty. Will she have the courage to strike out on her own and leave? Or will she be sitting here when spring comes, still dithering?

Her thoughts are interrupted by Dominic, calling from the patio. 'What year did we meet? How old were you?' He holds a pad and pen, ready to make a note.

She wanders back to the patio reluctantly. 'Have you finished your childhood already?'

'I didn't put all that much in about my childhood. Privileged and indulged. Brutalised at boarding school. Semi-comatose through university. Common story, no point in dwelling on that part. I always loathe having to read about people's childhoods: self-indulgent twaddle.'

'Why not leave me out of it, Dominic?' She picks up the yard broom distractedly and begins to sweep the dead leaves into a pile.

'Susannah, it's a tell-all. Think of it as plundering the past to fund the future.'

'It all seems rather sordid now – I don't want to go through all that again. Please, haven't I put up with enough?'

'It's not *sordid*, you silly woman, it's colourful. You're seeing it through the filter of your own dreary conventionality.'

'It attracted enough attention from the so-called gutter press at the time, I think that says something.'

'Well, that's the point. Context. Besides, times have changed. All that's all tame now, wouldn't even make the papers.'

'I'll be curious as to how you contextualise this most recent episode, destroying innocent people's lives.'

'Don't knock yourself out about that. It's all raw clay to be shaped by an incisive writer.' He pauses a moment and she senses his gaze on her. 'At least I'm *doing* something, which is better than sitting around in a semi-coma dabbing up the odd stray tear. But since you are so curious, I'm calling it *Confessions of a Critic*. Everything goes in. Every last detail. The champagne-drenched years – actually, that's not a bad chapter title. Lots of food . . . sex . . . in fact, you could help with some juicy bits. I can barely remember what goes where now. Who was that willowy blonde with the spider tattoo, our little playmate for a while there . . . did she become someone?'

'I don't remember, Dominic. And I don't care to remember. What are you going to say about Mr Farash? You won't get away with making up some nonsense that lets you off the hook . . .'

'We all make our own decisions in life, Susannah. You can't make someone else responsible for your life . . . or death.' He gazes out into the middle distance, across the field to the bare woods. 'Mr Farash made his decision and he took the cowardly way out.'

There have been times in the past when she fantasised about waking up in the morning and finding Dominic gone, perhaps dead but not necessarily – permanently missing would be sufficient. She wouldn't put up posters offering a reward, she would just stoically accept his disappearance. She could ask a few people if they've seen him, just to show some interest. But those fantasies were usually an overwrought response to a particular incident. Now she's seized with the urge to take matters into her own hands, and damn the consequences.

She has a vision of Mr Farash's kind face, his mischievous smile. Always so courteous and friendly. And sweet Mrs Farash, and the children, so polite. The whole family worked so hard only to have their lives destroyed by a sweep of Dominic's hand. She feels a blind rage, like a hot flush, like the mother of all hot flushes, surge through her body. Her vision is reduced to a tunnel, at the end of which she can only see Dominic and his insufferable smugness.

Without conscious thought, she swings the broom wildly in his direction. She catches him by surprise but the first blow is awkward, lacking force, and he manages to deflect it with his elbow. He gives a surprised grunt, but before he has time to retaliate, she adjusts her grip. Using the broom as a stave, she executes a double-handed swing with her full force into his ribs where it lands with a satisfying crack and elicits a cry of pain from him. The next one is for Mrs Farash! In a single movement the broom loops upwards and slams down hard on his shoulder. Up again, as high as her reach allows, she imagines it splitting his skull in two like a melon but a moment of hesitation allows him to gather his wits. Clutching his ribs, he hobbles off inside the house towards the safety of his study and its locking door. Left behind, Susannah thrashes about ineffectually whacking at the furniture, sobbing with frustration and terrifying the pugs, until she runs out of steam.

Drained by her exertions, she walks slowly back to the arbour seat and sits down. She tries to make sense of the last few minutes. Never in her life has she lashed out at anyone, verbally or physically. The idea of actually hurting someone is abhorrent to her. She's terrified for her own mental state. She has to stop thinking and start acting. She has to make things happen. Stop fighting Dominic and fight her way out.

Knowing he is not foolish enough to venture out of his study in the near future, she goes inside and quietly edges the Jacobean chair out of the living room into the kitchen. From there she hefts it out the kitchen door and down the side of the house. She flips down the rear seats of the car and, with much effort, manages to get it on its side in the back of the car, and covers it with a blanket. She slips back inside for her coat, handbag and the dogs and sets off immediately for Toulouse.

Chapter Twenty-one

Dominic sits at his desk, wrapped up in a duvet, his breath hanging in the air. The fire splutters fitfully, offering no relief from today's bitter chill. He can hear Susannah outside, sweeping the path at the front of the house. She seems to have formed an unhealthy attachment to that yard broom. But he is hardly going to bring that to her attention given the wretched woman's murderous behaviour yesterday.

Post-assault, she disappeared off somewhere. Hopefully to seek medical help. Perhaps they gave her something because last night she seemed perfectly calm and cooked a decent meal for a change, which they ate in separate rooms. She had rearranged the living-room furniture, an activity most women seem to find soothing, and obviously did a decent job since the room felt somehow more spacious.

Neither of them has mentioned her crazy behaviour or spoken a word to each other, for that matter. Clearly no apology is forthcoming. He is still in acute pain from the blows she inflicted on him, his shoulder sore and a nasty shade of purple. His ribs are either badly bruised or fractured if that cracking sound was anything to go by. It certainly hurts like hell when he breathes, which is painfully often. Nothing a few painkillers and the occasional Scotch can't deal with – he isn't going to be deterred from his quest by a few twinges. Thank God there is absolutely no risk of him laughing in the near future. That would be excruciating.

Ten pages into his manuscript and he's already cursing himself for not having a computer. This typing lark is ridiculous. Mechanically banging each letter onto each page when other people are able to dispatch their work around the world in seconds. It is simply the way he's always done it. Computers had come into play while he was a food columnist but, because of his celebrity, the paper had indulged him and provided a copy taker. It wasn't as though it was difficult for them to key in six hundred words. In the old days stringers and correspondents all called in their stories to the desk. News copy was one step up from stream of consciousness: who, what, why, when, where, add a cliché or two and a bit of actual news, if it existed at all. His column was far more exacting. Every word had to be precise, every sentence finessed; every paragraph a story in itself. His structure was always the same: a brazen or outrageous first paragraph to hook the reader, followed by a more exploratory even-handed one that set the scene, then a nuanced critique of the food, all tied together with a pithy summation. A complete dish in itself: engaging, amusing, a little spice and seasoning, garnished with a perfectly chosen adjective or two but without unnecessary embellishment.

He rarely wasted time commenting on decor or atmosphere as these were, to some extent, a matter of personal taste. Besides, critiquing the decor of restaurants in Britain would be shooting fish in a barrel. He had a particular loathing of anything resembling a 'theme' but was aware that many places he felt lacked a single redeeming visual feature, the hoi polloi considered utterly charming. The French had the right idea in this regard: pack as many patrons as possible into a small shabby room in which the decor has never been updated – ever!

As he pecks away at his typewriter, fingers stiff with cold, body aching from the blows of the previous day, it begins to dawn on him that he is a heroic figure, pushing on undaunted and undefeated towards his goal. Perhaps he can incorporate this endeavour into his future author talks, travelling the country – the world! – inspiring others to tell their stories, although preferably not to him. He might have to tone it down a bit, though; perhaps reconfigure his current injuries as an accident. Although, Susannah might be sectioned by then, so he'd be free to talk about her looney behaviour with impunity. In fictional terms he is a Jane Eyre persona being terrorised by the wife in the attic, or on the patio, in this case. Although, in fact, the mad wife is *his* wife, which makes him the long-suffering Rochester character.

Susannah's increasingly erratic behaviour is not just a distraction but a bloody worry. She's always had the potential for derangement and frequently insists it's *him* making her crazy. Perhaps she's festering a real mental illness, or even dementia? 'Early onset' seems to be the term on everyone's lips these days. Yes, they are in dire straits but it's hard to conceive that someone could get quite so overwrought about a financial situation. One that will naturally right itself, eventually. And it's not as though he isn't trying to help it along by being productive and getting on with things.

He wonders exactly how long the book should be. Hugging the duvet around him, one hand clamped on his tender ribcage, he gets up from his desk and searches the shelves for an unambitious-sized volume. A quick calculation suggests around seventy thousand words. He does the arithmetic on a scrap of paper and discovers that's the equivalent of writing just over one hundred and sixteen columns. Put that way it seems a little wearing but achievable, especially since he doesn't have to dine out one hundred and sixteen times in order to write about it. Actually, inserting ten of his best reviews would equal around six thousand words, and subtracted from seventy thousand equals sixty-four thousand. Less the couple of thousand or so he has already written and he only has sixty-odd thousand words to go.

What sort of advances are publishers paying these days? An upfront commitment would give him the requisite kick in the pants. He thinks of all the people he knows with some connection to publishing and notes down half-a-dozen names, then crosses off the ones who probably would not take a call from him. One name remains: Martin Marlborough. While Martin probably has as much reason to bear a grudge as the others, it just isn't in his nature.

He finds Martin's details in the Rolodex and is halfway through dialling when he realises there's no dial tone. How the hell is he supposed to sell the blasted book without a telephone? He screws up the piece of paper and throws it in the fire. The slight twisting movement sends a dagger of pain through his torso. He takes a slug of Scotch and feels the liquid warming his atrophied limbs. As he begins to tap gamely at the keys, he feels for a brief moment more like Hemingway than Rochester.

Chapter Twenty-two

The villa has a long, narrow attic and it's empty apart from a few boxes that look as if they were left here when the house was sold. One box is neatly packed with records, mostly flat LP size but also some cylindrical ones, mainly classical music, but no record player. Other boxes contain books and magazines. Not as interesting as I might have hoped – it seems like whoever packed them just didn't have the heart to throw them away.

I carry the boxes downstairs and unpack the contents onto the table in the summer room, which is not very summery right now but not too bad with the heating and warm clothes on. The books are mostly French classics: Flaubert, Voltaire, Guy de Maupassant and Camus, all beautifully leather-bound, and I feel some satisfaction in replacing them on the book shelves where they belong.

The doorbell clangs and I open it to find Enzo, the electrician's offsider, standing on the doorstep. He refuses my invitation to come in, but says he needs a word with Monsieur Tinker. I message Ben and a moment later he comes downstairs and we embark on a difficult conversation. It seems that Enzo has been sent by Monsieur Morel to collect three hundred euro outstanding on the account.

'Tell him that's not right, it's fully paid,' says Ben.

In a bold move, Enzo decides to break out his English. 'Non. This . . . hmm, *supplémentaire* . . . *matériaux* . . . *câbles* . . . Monsieur Harrington say he pay. He does not. You pay, Monsieur Tinker.'

'He's saying that the materials —'

'Yes, I get it,' Ben interrupts me. Worse, he launches into French: 'But Monsieur Morel wrote . . . *écrit* . . . the . . . *le euro* . . . on a piece of paper . . . what's a piece of paper? *Papier* . . . ahhh . . . *en tranche* . . . Where the hell is that bit of paper?'

Enzo's increasingly pained expression is not helping Ben find the words he needs.

'Ben, stop – you're just confusing things,' I say quietly. '*En tranche* is a slice, not a piece. Please, let me do this?'

'Fine.' And without another word, he goes back upstairs.

Now we speak in French and Enzo explains that it was Monsieur Morel's idea that he speak directly with Monsieur Tinker, not his, so now he can speak freely. 'I think there was a miscommunication about the estimate from the beginning,' he explains. 'It only covered the labour for the job, not the materials. I have been to the Harringtons' house three times, but they don't answer the door. So . . . this is where it lands. Monsieur Morel is retired, and he only agreed to do the job because Harrington already owed him money. He thought he was going to get paid; he didn't expect to be owed more at the end of it.'

'Of course we will pay the three hundred. I don't understand why Monsieur Harrington would have done that. We should have paid it right from the beginning. It's not his responsibility. If you can come back, maybe tomorrow, we'll have the cash for you. And please tell Monsieur Morel that we're sorry, we really had no idea.'

'Very good. Thank you. That Harrington – *phuff* – he's like a rooster, always crowing about something. Typical roastbeefs. I prefer Australians,' he says with a wink as he turns away.

When he's gone, I go upstairs to see what's bothering Ben, who is now back on his computer as if nothing happened. 'I've told him we'll give him the cash tomorrow.'

'Cool,' he says without taking his eyes off the screen.

'So what do you reckon that was about? Why would Dominic do that?'

'Don't know. Embarrassed that he made a mistake?'

'I guess so, but he could have just admitted it. Seems ridiculous.'

Ben glances up at me. 'Or honourable. He guaranteed the quote.'

'I suppose so. It's a lot of money and our responsibility.'

Ben taps away on his keyboard as if waiting for me to leave. 'You don't always have to think the worst of him, you know.'

'Ben, are you okay? I've told you I can help you more with your French, if that's what's upsetting you.'

'I don't really want to be one of your students.'

'No, I know . . . but . . .'

He gives a sigh and pushes his chair back from the desk. 'Sorry. It's just so frustrating. I feel like I'm only half here, and the other half is over there on the project. When this is done, I'll start proper lessons. Okay?'

I kiss the top of his head. He's never mad for long.

As I turn away, I catch sight of a figure hurrying across the fields. After a moment I realise that it's Susannah. She comes closer, practically running along our perimeter wall like a fugitive. Ben's monitors block his view but he notices me looking at something and asks what's up. Some instinct to protect Susannah makes me tell him it's nothing, and I hurry downstairs to open the front door before she rings the bell.

She's clutching an overnight bag to her chest and looking wrung out. 'Oh, don't worry, I haven't come to stay,' she says, attempting a feeble laugh. 'I did want to ask a favour, though.' She glances down the road. 'Was that the electrician's mate I saw leaving?'

'Yes, we're just settling the last of the bill. All taken care of now.' I catch a look of relief on her face. It's difficult to believe that the dishevelled-looking woman standing on my doorstep is the same one who arrived in that stunning blue dress only a couple of months ago. Bundled up in layers of shabby clothes, she looks grey and haggard. I invite her in, make us both tea and take her to the summer room.

'I wouldn't ask you this if I wasn't absolutely desperate. I just can't think of any other solution. I don't know what you'll think of me . . .' Susannah opens the bag to reveal four bottles of wine wrapped up in tea towels. 'Do you think it would be possible to sell these on the internet?'

'Of course, I can put them on eBay for you. Or there are probably dedicated sites for auctioning wine. Let's have a look . . .' I sit down at my computer and do a quick search. 'Actually, let me just see if there's any indication of prices.'

Susannah sits quietly watching me as I key in the details of the first bottle. She keeps glancing uneasily at the door. 'Is Ben here?'

'He's working upstairs, why?'

'Dominic doesn't know. You won't tell, will you? Some are worth a lot more than others. I just selected a few at random.'

To keep a secret from Dominic, I'll also have to keep it from Ben. How can I refuse when she's clearly so desperate? 'Shouldn't you talk to Dominic about it? I mean, if you really need the money . . . Susannah, this Chateau Michaud is worth seven hundred euros!'

Susannah leans towards me, the words tumbling out of her. 'Mia, we're living in poverty with a gold mine in the cellar . . . there's no money for food . . . heating . . . Dominic has no sense of reality. He thinks money comes and goes magically . . . he thinks I'm being hysterical. I am hysterical! With worry. That restaurant he wanted to take you to – Grégoire's – it's the most expensive restaurant in Toulouse, we'd be lucky to get out for under eight hundred euros. The cards are full, the bank's empty . . . he can't seem to grasp that. And then that business with the electrician . . . I'm so sorry . . . I feel terribly embarrassed.'

Feeling a strange mix of compassion, obligation and general awkwardness, I reach out to give her a comforting pat, only to find my hand firmly clasped.

'I have no one to turn to. Not a soul. The Van den Bergs probably told you we have no friends here. Not one. Dominic offended so many people, they closed ranks on us . . .'

'Susannah, the Van den Bergs are lovely people . . . they —'

'Of course they are! They're all lovely, it's not them!'

'Listen, leave the bottles with me. I can put them up for auction and let you know how it goes.'

'Oh, I'd be so grateful if you could. So grateful.'

'You need to give me your bank account details – I can open the auction account in your name and —'

'Is that necessary? I don't really want . . . couldn't you give me the cash?'

'If the money goes into our joint account, Ben's going to ask questions. Also the wine doesn't belong to me. If Dominic finds out I could be accused of stealing. I want to help you, Susannah, but I don't want to get into legal trouble.'

'No, no, of course not. I'm sorry. Is there any way around it at all? No? All right. I'll bring you the details or perhaps I'll call you. I have to be so careful.'

'I'll get it all set up in your name and wait for your details.' I pause. 'Are you sure that you want to do this?'

Susannah nods blindly, desperately. She wraps up the bottles carefully and puts them back in the bag. 'Better keep these some-where . . . you know . . . hidden.'

She heaves a sigh as though a weight has been lifted off her shoulders, and looks about her. 'This is such a beautiful room. So spacious and light.' She picks up a book off the table, giving it a cursory look. 'Shame they're not in English, it's so hard to get books here. You've probably realised by now that I don't speak French at all, apart from a word or two. It's a wonder Dominic hasn't brought it up yet, he likes to make a joke of it. I have tried. I just don't . . . perhaps it's confidence . . . I don't know. It doesn't seem to stick.'

'It's not easy, Ben's having a hard time of it too. When we were growing up, Eva only spoke to us kids in French. I loved the language and loved speaking a different language. But when they got to high school, both my brothers decided it was embarrassing and pretended not to understand. It's so much harder to learn when you're older.'

'Let alone ancient like me,' adds Susannah.

I touch her arm. 'Don't be so hard on yourself.'

The line of her mouth tightens. 'Actually, I think the time has come to be harder on myself. I've been too easy on myself. Too compliant and let things slide. I need to toughen up. I better go . . . I'm so sorry to drag you into this.'

'I can let you out the side gate, if you're going home cross-country.'

'Oh God, you saw me. I just didn't want . . . how awful for you . . . you must have wondered . . .'

'It's fine,' I assure her.

We leave by the French doors and cross the garden. I open the gate that leads out to the back fields. She looks so pitiful, poor woman. I give her a hug and she fixes me with a tragic look. 'Mia, you don't have to come to us for Christmas. I wouldn't blame you if you didn't want to.'

'We'll be there. I promise.'

Susannah smiles but it fades quickly and she looks worried. 'One other thing: you know recently Ben's come up to have coffee with Dominic a few times. I don't think . . . I don't know . . . just be careful, will you?' And with that she sets off across the paddock, hugging her coat to her against the cold wind.

Chapter Twenty-three

Trying to be practical, Susannah makes lists. She writes a new list every day, but will then uncover an almost identical list she doesn't recall writing. Surrounded by plans but no further ahead. The prospect of leaving France terrifies her for countless reasons that weigh her down and infiltrate her dreams. Fear lands with a thump on her chest in the night and she wakes with a shudder, gasping for air. The spectre of being alone in the world clutches at her heart. She sees herself lying among dank, stained sheets, in a dusty room, incapacitated and forgotten. Slipping from this world to the next without a comforting hand to guide her. No one to hear her last sigh. No one mourning her death.

She's acutely aware that every problem she faces will be her problem, her responsibility alone. She married Maxwell at twenty-two; she has always been someone else's responsibility. In her more rational moments, she reasons that Dominic is the cause of most of her problems and she is responsible by default. She tries to count her blessings but they seem insubstantial – not enough to see her through. As she often does in desperate times, she makes a mental list of the people who love her: Lou and Chou, Maxwell and Reggie. Rebecca loves her grudgingly and Simon tolerates her – so they only count for half each. Dominic does not feature on the list. It doesn't seem a lot to be going on with but it's something. Perhaps there are other friends in London who will allow her back into their lives if she's on her own.

While she's not proud of attacking Dominic with a broom, it made her realise that she is teetering on the brink. With Mia's support, she feels a little more stable and has had to forcibly restrain herself from apologising to him in an attempt to make things more pleasant. He needs to know that she has a limit.

Nestled beside her in bed, the dogs now leap up, yapping frantically. Susannah pulls her coat on over her pyjamas, pushes her feet into slippers and goes out to the top of the stairs. She can hear someone knocking on the front door. Dominic must be able to hear it from his study!

As she rushes downstairs to open the door, she's aware how neglected the house looks. The kitchen has dirty dishes piled on the benches. The fireplace hasn't been cleaned in days and the living room stinks of wet ash. It's probably just Monsieur Bonnet who lives further down the lane. He has a great regard for the British that harks back to the war and occasionally rewards them with vegetables from his garden. Ben doesn't use the front door. Dominic practically lives in his study these days, so it's easier for Ben to tap on the French windows and enter the room directly from the courtyard. What Susannah is not expecting to see is a young woman clad in jeans, boots and a puffer jacket. Her blonde hair is in a topknot, and there are silver hoops in her ears. English.

'Yes?' asks Susannah as the pugs rush through her legs to bark at the stranger. She's assuming the woman is lost since her car is visible, pulled off to the side of the lane.

'You must be Susannah. I'm Roxanne.'

Susannah feels her whole body go limp; she clutches the door jamb for support. It's as though she has always known this day would come, without ever having consciously thought about it. As if she's dreaded it and forgotten it at the same time. How had she found them? Why now, when it feels as though life could barely get any worse? On top of everything else, Susannah is mentally wringing her hands at the state of the house. 'I suppose you better come in,' she says faintly.

They stand in the hallway. Unnervingly self-contained, Roxanne looks around curiously. She bends down and offers her hand to the dogs for their approval. 'So sweet. What are their names?'

'Lou-Lou and Chou-Chou.' The names sound twee and juvenile to Susannah's own ears.

'Oh, gorgeous,' says Roxanne without enthusiasm. 'Is he here?'

They're standing right beside the closed door of the study; there is no way to forewarn Dominic. Susannah taps gently on the door and calls his name, her voice quavery, like an old woman. 'There's someone here to see you.' She gives Roxanne a reassuring smile. There is no telling what Dominic's response to this visitor will be.

'How many times do I have to tell you not to disturb me?' he shouts back.

Susannah opens the door. 'Roxanne's here to see you, *darling*.' The endearment forces its way out like something thickly putrid caught in her throat.

Dominic looks up from his typewriter, a wreath of smoke suspended above him. He gave up smoking years ago to preserve his tastebuds but has taken it up again, insisting it helps him concentrate. He stares at Susannah and then at Roxanne over the top of his glasses, looking from one to the other for enlightenment. Susannah realises she is quite enjoying seeing him caught on the back foot. Roxanne also seems in no hurry to ease the awkwardness in the room. She stands gazing at him as though at a deity, her expression one of quiet wonder and jubilation.

'It's me. Roxy.'

Susannah watches the slow dawning of recognition on Dominic's face. There's a flicker of something – fear or guilt? – immediately replaced by his usual response to anything unexpected: annoyance. 'How did you get here?' he asks.

'She has a car,' offers Susannah, gesturing out the window helpfully.

'After an unexplained absence from his daughter's life for over thirty years, his first words to her are: "How did you get here?"' Roxy sounds amused more than anything.

Dominic stands up slowly, taking care to nurse his injured ribs. Not, it seems, to greet or embrace his daughter, but to address the psychological disadvantage. 'How did you find me?'

'It wasn't that difficult. You'd obviously changed your name, but I was able to track down Susannah's sister quite easily, and she was more than happy to give me your address.'

Dominic shoots Susannah a furious look as though her family are conspiring against him.

'Did your mother send you?' asks Dominic.

'I'm a little too old to be sent places by my mother. No, it was my idea alone. She doesn't know anything about it. I wanted to meet you. Found out your address and drove here. Simple as that.'

'So, now what?' he asks. 'Is there more to the plan?'

Roxy laughs out loud. 'You're exactly as I imagined you.'

Susannah's quietly impressed by Roxy's apparent imperviousness to her father's hostility. Lou and Chou seem to like her and hang around, gazing up with interest.

'Well, I wouldn't mind a cup of tea,' says Roxy with a smile.

'That seems achievable.' Dominic raises a commanding eyebrow in Susannah's direction.

She pulls the armchair up close to his desk for his visitor. 'You two have a little catch-up while I make the tea.'

Roxy sits down, head high, eyes fixed on Dominic, like a queen ascending to the throne. Nerves of steel by the looks of her.

Twenty minutes later, Susannah opens the door to the study, balancing the tea tray against her hip, breathless from the exertion of pelting around the house throwing mess into cupboards, clearing the benches and piling all the dishes will-nilly into the dishwasher. She still wears her pyjamas under her coat, having had no time to change.

Dominic sits typing at his desk, a fresh cigarette balanced on his lip. Without looking up, he asks: 'What year did . . . oh, never mind. Your memory is even worse than mine.'

Susannah looks wildly around the room, almost dropping the tray. 'Where is she?'

'Oh, she just left. Ben turned up, so I sent her off with him. I need to get this chapter finished. She's booked into a hotel up the top.'

Susannah has a sudden vision of herself as a foolish old

woman in a shabby coat, standing there stupidly holding a tray of tea that no one wants.

Dominic glances up. 'What? It's not as though we have room for her. She'll come down for a drink later.' He begins to type, tapping away with two fingers, feigning immersion in his work.

'Well . . . how long is she staying?'

'A week or so, I believe. Now, can I get on? It's impossible to concentrate with all these interruptions.'

'She's not Ben's responsibility . . .'

'Look, Susannah, far be it from me to intuit your tangled logic but she has turned up here uninvited and unannounced, so as far as I'm concerned she's no one's responsibility. And tell that sister of yours to stop blabbing about our whereabouts or, next thing we know, we'll have the press banging on the door.'

Susannah grips the tray so tightly that the cups rattle in their saucers and tea slops out of the pot. Not trusting herself, she rushes for the door.

'By the way, I invited her to spend Christmas with us.'

'What?! Oh, Dominic, really?'

'Anyway, they're back for drinks at five. So you can discuss it with her yourself. Shut the door, will you, it's bloody draughty. Hoy! Where are you going with that tea!'

Chapter Twenty-four

Meeting Roxy was a peculiar experience. Dominic felt no particular connection with her, no rush of fatherly warmth or even a sense of recognition. In fact, her name meant nothing at all to him initially. It was only the expression on Susannah's face that jogged his memory. He wouldn't have picked her as his daughter to look at – she doesn't resemble Michelle, but definitely has a helping of chutzpah he could lay claim to.

It's uncanny that the girl should turn up right now. He'd been jumping from one era to another, writing the bits he remembers, gratified to discover tiny vistas of memory beckoning him on into the distance, revealing things he'd forgotten. He's realised that writing about the past is like wandering into a cinema when the lights are down: it's counterproductive to stumble around flailing for something to hold on to. One has to be patient and wait for one's vision to adjust. He's uncovered solid nuggets of story; some of the detail is lost, but a little extrapolation here and there is bringing it vividly to life.

What a treat to wander through the riotous years revisiting

Madame Jojo's, Raymond's Revue and The Marquee. Nights that went on for days with well-known names sprinkled throughout like stardust. So energising to relive those filthy alcohol-sodden nights of red-blooded fun. It all starts to get rather tame when Michelle appears on the scene, though. She quietened him down for a year or two – he was probably in need of some rest – but he was never one to miss out on the fun for long. He's reluctantly decided to bestow pseudonyms on all his lovers, especially during his time with Michelle – keep the punters guessing and avoid being sued. Apart from one or two, they are all respectable matrons these days. First and foremost he has a responsibility to the truth, apart from the odd detail he might need to fabricate to make it more interesting and lucid.

The seventies and eighties; just the thought of those two decades gives him a rush of nostalgia. Back then he believed it would go on forever. When you're having the time of your life, it's not as though you look ahead and wonder if one day you'll end up living in a brutally cold house in a foreign country with a woman desperately in need of psychiatric help. You think the good times will continue to roll. He had money back then. Not fabulous wealth, but more than enough to live the high life. These days people seem to cultivate an aversion to money, as though it is something incidental; of no importance. Back then, people quite rightly worshipped the stuff. Back then it was acknowledged as the key to everything good in life. He had driven cars that were better than sex. Sex! There was a ridiculous amount of sex. In the sixties 'free love' was a theory. In the seventies women started putting it into practice. Underwear went missing for at least a decade, apart from slithery little numbers called teddies. There was a smorgasbord of women to choose from. Then, for some inexplicable reason, perhaps weary of feasting, his palate desirous of something simple and nourishing for a change, he married Michelle. They were a cliché of the eighties: they smoked pot, drank Harvey Wallbangers and married impulsively.

There was a remote possibility that a loosely woven marriage might have worked but the wedding vows activated a primal switch in Michelle's brain and she jumped tracks. Turned out that the whole bohemian business was a front for a woman deeply entrenched in suburban sensibilities. She wanted them to move out of his Notting Hill flat and buy a house near her parents in Walthamstow. Walthamstow! On the edge of the known universe. Here be dragons. He dug his heels in. She campaigned. He stayed out late. She waited up. It was relentless. After months of bickering, he agreed to try Camden Town, which was just the right side of the suburban wastelands. He stonewalled on the actualities of the relocation. She got pregnant. He met Susannah.

Susannah's husband, Maxwell Dixon, was the darling of the West End. Every show he directed was a smash. He was wooed by actors and producers alike. He neglected his wife, which was a mistake because she was beautiful. Gorgeous. Irresistible. Hard to believe it now, but Susannah was the most uninhibited woman he'd ever encountered. They were either drunk or getting drunk; either screwing or thinking about screwing. They were indiscreet and utterly obsessed with each other. But when the cuckolded twigged to the situation, they joined forces and came at the lovers from every direction. The director turned the whole episode into a tragic drama with himself in the starring role. Michelle competed as the untamed shrew.

By that time Dominic didn't have the stomach for conflict he'd once had. Ironically he and Susannah ended up renting a place together in Camden and, once their divorces came through, married, almost as if to prove it was all worthwhile. After all Susannah had suffered, Reggie felt the urge to come to the rescue and bought the house for her. Dominic was soon poached by an opposition paper and their life of abundance resumed. Maxwell and Susannah had made peace but Michelle never forgave him, which makes Roxy's appearance all the more surprising.

She had been presenting him with a problem even before she manifested. It was almost as though she sensed his dilemma and turned up to force her own inclusion in his story. Leaving Michelle when she was pregnant would take some careful explanation, apart from stressing the obvious: that it was commonplace back then. It was the 1980s. Everyone did it. Back then liaisons dissolved and reassembled with different players quite effortlessly.

Michelle obviously had her own part to play in his defection. It wasn't as though she was screwing around, she was too busy titivating the flat and reading him passages from *The Female Eunuch*, which she embraced a full decade after everyone else had forgotten it. That book alone was enough to send him screaming out into the night. But then she got herself pregnant. And that was the end for him. Those bad-boy chefs got away with this sort of behaviour all the time. The problem remains that it makes him seem untrustworthy, which makes it harder to defend his innocent intentions over the Farash affair. Unless he can shake that one off, any hopes of this book springboarding him into a television career could be severely compromised.

He leaves his study and makes his way to the kitchen to forage for something edible. Pleasingly, Roxy's visit has spurred Susannah into action, because here she is scrubbing the worktops like someone possessed. Something is actually cooking in the oven, and the kitchen is warm and relatively inviting as a result. There's nothing much to snack on but he finds a loaf of thin sliced white bread in the freezer and puts two slices into the toaster.

'What are you going to do about her?' asks Susannah, jerking around to face him. 'You can't just fob her off onto Ben.'

'What do you suggest? She's met me, basked in my radiance, probably all she wanted. I did invite her for Christmas, but got the impression that you object to that.'

'If she's here for a week, you have to do something. Make her welcome. Do you want her going back and telling Michelle we're living in squalor and poverty?'

'Or that this was recently the scene of a serious domestic violence incident?' asks Dominic, mildly. 'There's no shame in a little genteel poverty, but *that* was something else again.'

'Dominic, please don't provoke me. You must see that I am at the very end of what I can deal with. I can't bear to hear you dismissing what happened to Mr Farash so lightly . . . you don't seem to understand that a man is dead because of you —'

'Susannah, for Christ's sake, everything doesn't have to be part of your ongoing melodrama. Farash is gone and nothing can bring him back. A little untidiness is hardly squalor. Our minor financial hiccup, most likely due to your poor management, will be resolved in due course. Let's revisit my original question: What do you suggest?'

He remembers a time when Susannah's face was guileless, untroubled by any hint of serious thought. Now he watches her features twist into a parody of anger and frustration; a snarling fishwife. Her crazy behaviour is no aberration, it's just the way some women turn out.

Not bothering to answer him, she turns back to the sink, shaking her head in disgust; and begins to scrub her hands furiously under the water. What a sight she is, hunched over the sink, the saggy pants of her pink flannelette pyjamas hanging below her coat and ugly old-woman slippers broken at the back because she's too slovenly to put them on properly. She insisted on separate rooms from the day they moved into this house and when he looks at her now he's almost grateful for his enforced state of celibacy. It's hard to imagine that there was a time when she was irresistible to him. He'd always been a buttock man. The sight of a hip-hugging dress taut across her long haunches, the tantalising knowledge of the smooth alabaster beneath . . . He wonders, would she even have the power to arouse him now? Attacking him with that broom was the most interesting thing she'd done in years. And almost as he thinks it, he finds himself behind her at the sink. With one hand he grips the back of her neck, roughly shoving her head under the running water. With the other, he pulls her coat up over her shoulders and wrenches the pyjama pants down, exposing her naked buttocks. As he suspected, they are not as he remembers. The once firm white orbs are now shapeless and dimpled as cold porridge.

Disoriented under the stream of water, Susannah screams furiously, her arms flailing helplessly for the tap – or him – and finding neither. He has her firmly pinned against the bench and the pyjamas gathered around her knees hamper her attempts to kick him.

He's in no rush to release her despite the pain of his ribs, or perhaps because of the pain. He rubs himself against her naked buttocks experimentally. Nothing. He's had more thrills from a mouthful of decent *foie gras* on a nice thin slice of white toast. At that moment, his toast pops up and, feeling creative, he wedges one slice between her quivering buttocks. 'There you are,' he says cheerfully, munching on the other piece of toast. 'I've finally found a use for you.'

Chapter Twenty-five

Ben had been unaware that Dominic had a daughter, but was not all that surprised. He's often the last person to find things out and assumes he was distracted when everyone else was listening. In any case, he didn't need to know about Roxy and now he just needs to carry out his duty as Dominic's deputised host.

He had walked across the fields to the Harringtons', so goes with Roxy in her car to the village where they stop for *petit déjeuner* at the Salon de Thé. It's quiet this morning, just a few people out doing errands. Half-a-dozen men sit outside the bar opposite drinking *un express* from tiny white cups, their faces raised towards the winter sun. Ben explains the layout of the town, this lower part being the business centre with a dozen or so useful shops and Saturday market, whereas the old town up the hill is the touristy part with nothing useful to buy unless you're after handmade chocolates or *foie gras*.

Roxy was chirpy and confident at the Harringtons'; now she seems subdued. Ben tries to think about things from her point of view, a practice he has worked hard to perfect over the years, under the tutelage of both Mia and Olivia. 'It must have been nerve-racking coming to meet Dominic and Susannah,' he says as an opener.

'You have no idea. I haven't slept properly for days, just worrying about it. I haven't even been to my hotel yet – wanted to get the first meeting done with.'

'Oh well, the worst is over,' he assures her. 'If they were going to throw you out the door it would have happened by now.'

'That's one way of looking at it. Could still happen, I suppose. I'll just need to watch my step.'

'Dominic's bark is worse than his bite. He likes to overstate everything. He's really a decent guy.'

Roxy glances at him dubiously and looks away, as though she thinks it's an odd thing to say. If she doesn't think her father is a decent guy, then why is she even here?

'You've haven't known them long then?' she asks. 'Sorry, I haven't even asked you a thing about yourself. How rude of me!'

'That's okay, you're not here to see me. I'm just the tour guide.'

'It's not like you volunteered for the job.' She smiles.

'That's okay, I'm happy to show you round a bit. I was working until one this morning. It's nice to be outside. I go and have coffee with Dominic sometimes to get out of the house and talk to someone.'

After breakfast, they drive up the narrow cobbled laneways to the upper part of the village and park in one of the hotel spaces. Ben waits outside while she checks in.

As the sun slides up the twisting lanes and lights up the archways of each of the bastide walls, he thinks about the September evenings when he and Mia walked up here and he wonders if whatever they had recaptured back then was a sort of fantasy. It's like they were playing a part but now all the brightness seems to have faded, the life gone out of it.

When Roxy reappears, it takes a couple of blinks to recognise her. Her hair is loose around her shoulders, the bulky jacket exchanged for something lighter. Her face is bright with make-up. He doesn't really like make-up on women but, in any case, doesn't remember how she looked without it.

They walk along the lanes that encircle the town, stopping now and then to gaze out across the green plaid valley. Fields dotted with trees, the occasional house and little threads of roads stretching out to the distant hills. Ben keeps up a commentary of the history of the town: the wars, the plague, fortunes gained and lost. She's silent, so he assumes she's either interested or too polite to change the topic. They find themselves in a small park of oak trees, the ground covered in acorns, and sit down on one of the benches. The sun is soft and a strand of morning fog hangs suspended between the hill and the farms below, lifting them above the clouds.

'It's just unimaginably beautiful here,' says Roxy, gazing out across the valley. 'Like an illustration from a storybook. So peaceful. It's looks like it hasn't changed in hundreds of years.'

She's right. It is a magical place. The sort of place people dream about. The sort of place he and Mia dreamed about. And here it is, laid out at their feet. It's hard to imagine, sitting here basking in the sun – and Roxy's admiration of the place – why he's been feeling so disillusioned about it all.

'So, what brought you here? I suppose that's the standard question you get asked.'

'That's easy. My wife, Mia. Well, to be fair, she didn't make me. It was my idea.'

Ben knows that he often fails to pick up signals but he does notice Roxy's interest fade at the mention of Mia. Has he not mentioned Mia up to now? Maybe not. They're not one of those 'joined at the hip' couples who constantly reference each other. She just hasn't come up before now.

'Kids?' Roxy asks.

'Nope.'

She gives him a sideways look. 'Didn't want them?'

'No.' Ben pushes on, changing the subject. 'So, what made you come and find Dominic right now?'

'I guess a series of things. And, hey – if not now, when?'

'You don't hold it against him that he wasn't around when you were growing up?'

'Not really. He wasn't exactly welcoming today, though.'

Ben shrugs. 'He's a bit eccentric. You don't know how he's going to respond to anything.'

'I can see he really likes you; hopefully he'll feel the same way about me at some point.'

'I like him,' says Ben.

'So, your wife – Mia? – she won't mind you showing me the sights?'

Ben shakes his head. 'She doesn't worry about things like that.'

'Really? You must have been together a long time.'

'Hmm, fifteen years.'

'Are you serious? Wow, is that common in Australia?'

'Yeah, we only do monogamy. It's compulsory, like voting,' says Ben. 'Works for us.'

Roxy laughs. She has a decent sense of humour and it's a relief to have someone new to talk to – in English. In the last two weeks he's had conversations with exactly four people apart from Mia. Three months into the adventure and it's turning out to be duller than he could have ever imagined. He feels physically and mentally dormant. The most basic communication, outside the few people he knows, is painfully difficult and exhausting. He's starting to wonder if he's already too old to become fluent in a second language. But if they stay here, the last thing he wants is to be a second-class citizen, dependent on other people because of a communication disability.

'Look, I'm feeling bad for saying we didn't want kids. I was taking the easy way out,' says Ben out of the blue.

'Oh, I'm feeling horrible for asking. It's absolutely none of my business.'

'We did. A lot. But we couldn't. So that's it. And don't ask me whose fault it is —'

'God, I'm not *that* insensitive!'

'Plenty of people are. Anyway, we don't discuss that.'

'I'm so sorry. I feel terrible!' Roxy says.

'Forget it. Anyway, I'm going to head back and get some work done. I'll see you at Dominic's around five-ish for drinks.'

She reminds him to bring Mia and he agrees but already knows Mia won't want to go.

Chapter Twenty-six

Ben goes over to see Dominic practically every day now. To get out of the house – and away from me. I can't really blame him – we've never been together twenty-four hours a day before.

I don't mind walking alone. It's been raining the last few days but today is clear and bright, the cold sharp. I rug up warmly and go out every afternoon to walk around the nearby country-side. At the end of November there were still trees with bright yellow leaves, and long strands of ruby-red vines clinging to the stone walls and shutters. Now the colours are subdued, grass the colour of moss, bare trees like wisps of smoke. I love the changing of the seasons but I'm not sure how we'll get used to these long, cold winters.

Today I walk up rue la Peyrade to the town cemetery. Enclosed by mossy stone walls, *le cimetière* sits on the north side of the hill looking across the countryside towards our house. I've always loved cemeteries, a place where the dead and sometimes the living can find some peace. This one is small and mostly has family burial plots, small crypts with the family name carved in stone.

It doesn't take long to find *Famille Dupont*. Both the elder Duponts are buried here. Also in the family plot are their son, Antoine, who died in 1944; daughter, Mathilde Levant, who died four years ago; and her daughter, Esmée Levant, born in 1950, who died aged six. Esmée is our little girl. What tragedy took her life at only six? Is this what kept Madame Levant here all those years?

I leave the cemetery and walk on up to the village and the small shop that sells art and craft supplies to buy a new sketch pad and pencils that I really don't need. As I approach the shop, the woman in the brown hat, Madame Bellamy, walks out and goes off up the street. If I'd met her in the shop, I might have had a chance to talk with her. It's not so easy to engage with locals, especially older people. At home you can strike up a conversation anywhere with anyone. Here people are more guarded if you just start chatting; maybe being a foreigner makes it worse.

It's a nice little shop packed tight with every sort of art material, paints and canvases as well as craft items for making jewellery and wools and yarns. I greet the assistant, a woman about my age with thick dark hair pulled into a ponytail, and she returns the courtesy. I feel her eyes on me as I look around the shop. I find a good weight of sketch pad and a couple of soft graphite pencils and take them to the counter.

'You're the new owner of the house on rue Albert Bouquillon,' she says. 'The Australians.'

'We're famous, are we?' I smile.

She gestures towards the door. 'My mother – you may have seen her – she takes an interest. I heard you spoke good French.'

'Thank you; I'm not getting too much practice. I haven't really met any local people to have a conversation with. I'm Mia, by the way.'

'You can have a conversation with me. I'm Chloe,' she says, swapping to French as she puts my items in a paper bag. 'I went to Australia last year for three weeks, to Sydney. I loved it! You can come and talk with me any time.'

'Your mother, her name is Madame Bellamy?'

'Yes, do you know her?'

'I see her walk past the house.'

Chloe hesitates for a moment. 'My mother knew Madame Levant all her life. She spent a lot of time in that house. It was the end of an era for her. It's been very hard for her.'

'Did your mother know the daughter? Madame Levant's daughter, Esmée?'

She frowns. 'I'm not sure why you ask that but please don't ask my mother about this girl. We don't speak of her.'

'Oh, I'm so sorry. It was rude of me. I just . . . it's none of my business.'

'It's all right. You couldn't know. It's a sensitivity. But if you want to know about the house, I'm sure my mother would be happy to talk to you.' She hands me the package.

I give her my number and she promises to be in touch. We part with the usual *bonne journée* and I walk home feeling more curious than ever about the little girl.

Late in the afternoon, Ben comes into the summer room and stands looking at the books and records and china that was in the boxes, now spread all over the table. 'Come on, Mia-Cat, this stuff can wait. I think you should come over to the Harringtons and meet Roxy. She's expecting to meet you.'

I would like to put everything aside and go over to the Harringtons for a drink but I'm nervous about my covert operation with Susannah. I've sold more than a dozen bottles on her behalf, bringing in around four thousand euros. I didn't think it through properly when she asked me to do this, and I had no idea how much money would be involved. Now there's no turning back. Dominic probably has a couple of hundred bottles in his cellar but, the way he goes on, he seems to know them all intimately and it's only a matter of time before he notices one missing. Sooner or later, he has to figure it out.

The thought of him turning up here in a rage terrifies me. Ben would be furious with me too. He was a bit annoyed about the conversation at the Van den Bergs. He thinks that I should keep the chair story to myself because it wasn't that big a deal. He specifically asked me not to tell them about the situation with the electrician. It's weird the way he's so protective of Dominic. And undeserved, in my opinion. If there is anyone who can look after himself, it's Dominic.

'Why would she want to meet me?' I ask. 'I thought you said she only arrived this morning. Doesn't she want to have time with Dominic and Susannah? How do we fit in?'

'Well, just that we're good friends, I guess.'

'But they're family. If they've never met before, it's not like a normal social occasion. It doesn't make any sense to me.'

Ben shrugs. 'It does to me. Having someone else there makes it less awkward. Anyway, it's just a quick drink.'

'It's never just a quick drink with Dominic. You go, I'll get dinner ready for when you get back. Ben, don't you think it's strange that he never wanted to meet his own daughter?'

'Yeah. But he is odd. No surprises there. I don't understand why you're so down on him. It's not like we have any other friends here right now. Cut him some slack.'

'I don't understand why you're so keen on him. What do you talk about when you go over there?'

'Everything. His life. Wine. Food. His book.'

I look at him in disbelief. 'Anything that you're actually interested in?'

'I am interested,' says Ben, looking wounded. 'My dad was like that, just filling you up with information. He didn't have the sort of education Dominic has, but he was knowledgeable about loads of different subjects.'

I've never said a word to Ben, because he idolised his father, but everything I've ever heard about him makes me think he was one of those quiet controlling men. He ruled the family and everything had to be done his way. Olivia is older than Ben and she doesn't share the same rosy view of her father. Ben's mother tries to keep everyone happy but I doubt she's had too many happy times herself.

'Don't you think we need more friends closer to our age?'

He gives a defeated shrug. 'I guess. But where are they?'

The same old impasse. Around here anyone our age would be French; most of the English speakers are Brits and are of the Harringtons' vintage. But how long will it be before Ben can hold a real conversation in French? Two or three years? And that's with a lot of hard work.

*

It's late when Ben staggers into the bedroom and sits down heavily on the bed.

'What happened to you?'

'I messaged you. Yeah, sorry, one thing turned into another.' He tugs at his jumper, battling to get it over his head, but only gets halfway.

'Are you drunk? Is that mud all over your pants?'

'I got lost coming back across the paddock and fell over,' he says, flopping backwards on the bed, his head missing the pillow, his jumper trapped around his neck. 'I'll have to get the car in the morning.'

'Couldn't Roxy have given you a lift?'

'She's way too drunk to drive. She's still there. Dominic opened a . . . ah . . . Chateau Something or other and then something else . . .'

'I hope Roxy was impressed by all those Chateau Somethings. What about Susannah?'

'Susannah? What about her? What is the nature of your enquiry, madame?'

'Was she getting drunk too?'

He stares at the ceiling, getting his thoughts in order. 'Nah, didn't see her. Hiding upstairs. What time is it now?'

'Nearly ten.' I lean over and yank his jumper up over his head.

'*Shit*. I missed the scrum meeting. That's not good either. Lots of not-good things. Maybe a few good things. I'm not sure.'

'I can't remember seeing you this drunk in years; do you want a cup of tea or something?'

'I can get it.' Ben lifts his head and collapses back on to the bed. 'No. I can't.'

I get out of bed and pull my dressing-gown on. These days we keep the tea things in the bedroom to save going all the way downstairs to the kitchen. The milk stays cold on the windowsill.

I boil the kettle and bring a mug to Ben, helping position him semi-upright with a couple of pillows behind him. He takes the tea with a sweet drunken smile and wraps his frozen hands around the mug. His eyes drift closed and I just manage to grab the mug before he falls asleep.

Chapter Twenty-seven

In the privacy of her room, Susannah has begun to quietly sort out her belongings. The incident in the kitchen has hardened her resolve. Now there is no possibility whatsoever of staying here with that hateful, loathsome, vile man. She must make that bid for freedom and home.

She's determined that, over the next few days, she will play along pretending all is well while she completes her preparations. Christmas Day will be her last day in France. On Boxing Day she will find an opportunity to slip down to the cellar and pack a couple of dozen bottles. The minute Dominic is safely tucked away in his study working on his book of many lies, she will pack the car and leave.

Her resolve is strong but her hands tremble uncontrollably as she divides up her clothes, shoes, books, DVDs, photo albums and memorabilia into take or leave boxes. She has to be tough and decisive about the whole endeavour. She removes the dried bouquet of roses from its vase and throws it in the bin. Once she's home in England, she won't be reliant on her pathetic little ritual. After a moment she retrieves them. Maxwell went to the trouble to have them specially preserved for her. Few people in her life have been as thoughtful, so it does seem churlish to toss them. She wraps them in an old shirt and packs them away in a box.

The ideal of England as a green and promised land has grown in her imagination; she longs for her homeland as a soldier returning from war. The white cliffs are a siren call across the channel. Tears spring to her eyes at the thought. The idea of being in a country where she can be understood makes her feel giddy with relief. To not have people raise their voices in frustration or make that awful tutting noise when she can't understand them. She sees herself settled into Rebecca's little flat in Chiswick. Living her independent life. Pleasing herself what she does without having to endure Dominic's twenty questions about every decision. That is what's made her so indecisive, having to justify everything she does to him. Constantly bending to his will. Or was she always like that? Anyway, things will be different. She will rise above her circumstances. She'll become that strong, independent woman, heroic in her ability to overcome the hurdles put in her way. She just needs to get home.

Even though she loathes him with every fibre of her being, she feels a tiny bit guilty at leaving Dominic without a car. She could fly but she'd still have to get to Toulouse. Too complicated. If only she could be comfortable with being inconsiderate. Slipping away seems cowardly but at the same time essential. She can't face another filthy row dragging her back into everything she is determined to leave behind. And she knows that Dominic possesses the power to stop her, to undermine her and make her doubt any decision.

Tucked away in her handbag is a cheque from the English antique dealer in Toulouse who had included the Jacobean chair in a container going back to the UK where it sold at Sotheby's auction. Far from 'priceless', it did fetch a tidy sum that will be the foundation of her new life. He still hasn't noticed the chair has gone. She will pay the utility bills – he won't be left without electricity – and she'll put on a splendid Christmas Day feast, then take the money and run.

A dreadful thought occurs. Sometime in the next few days, Dominic will go down to the cellar to select the wine for Christmas Day. In his current mood, elevated by his fantasy of becoming a celebrated author (she overheard him discussing the film rights with Roxy recently), he's quite likely to want to push the boat out. She's tried to select from different parts of the cellar, so he won't notice the odd bottle missing, but should he decide on a particular wine and find it gone . . . she shudders at the thought. That simply can't happen. An interim plan is needed.

She has to watch her step with Roxy. So unfortunate that she's turned up right now. Susannah doesn't blame herself for what happened back then – it's not as though she had any idea that Michelle was pregnant. The two women had met socially on a couple of occasions, before Susannah and Dominic were outed. Roxy is nothing like her mother. Michelle has a trusting sweetness about her, or she did back then; that may have changed. But Roxy is different – there's something secretive about her. She appears to be enamoured with her father but it's impossible to tell whether it's genuine or not. She's certainly enamoured with Ben.

All the packing and disruption is making Lou and Chou unsettled. They sniff anxiously around the piles of folded clothes, stacks of books and her precious DVDs, all set out on the floor. 'We're going home, my little darlings,' she murmurs. 'Back where we belong. We're going to be fine. Absolutely fine.' The shrill of the phone beside the bed gives her a nasty start. She picks it up with trepidation.

'Susannah, it's Becky.'

'Oh, Becky, I've been meaning to call you. I'm coming home. For good.' Susannah drops her voice, gripped by the panicky thought that Dominic may have heard the phone ring. If he picks up the downstairs extension she will hear it click.

'That's good, Susie. But I'm sorry to have to be the bearer of bad news.'

Susannah sits down on the bed. Daddy. Remorse and regret wash over her. She should have gone home earlier. She will never be able to forgive herself for not seeing him during this last year. And now it's too late.

'I'm afraid our dear Maxwell died last night,' says Rebecca. 'His heart, they think. He's been under a lot stress. I was worried the last time we saw him, he didn't look well. Grey in face.'

Susannah feels as though she's accelerating towards an immovable object, powerless to stop or turn away. One moment she's distraught at losing her father and the next, grappling with the fact that it's Maxwell who's gone. The man she loved and lost, the man who adored her and was a shining beacon of her future. Gone. There had been no doubt in her mind that he would find her a part and that she would embark on the final phase of her career. She hadn't realised how wedded she was to this notion until this very moment.

'Susie? Are you there? I'm so sorry. I know you were still very fond of him.'

'But I just spoke to him, a couple of weeks ago . . . it's not possible.'

'Well, darling, he was alive a couple of weeks ago. He was alive yesterday, in fact. But now he's not. You're in shock. Spare a thought for Cynthia and the children. His family adored him, you know. The children are theatre people, all of them. Terribly sad. When are you back? The funeral will be next week.'

'Oh. The funeral . . . I'm not sure . . . I was going to come on Boxing Day.'

'Wonderful. We'll all be pleased to have you home. Alone, I presume?'

'Yes. Alone. Is it possible . . . do you still have that little flat you mentioned?'

'Chiswick? I've put a tenant in there now. You should have let me know. Never mind, Daddy has a spare room. He'll be happy to have you there for a little while. I'll let him know to expect you.'

Susannah hears herself agree to this plan as though from a great distance. When Rebecca hangs up, Susannah feels utterly abandoned and alone. She sits cradling the phone, wishing she could be channelled through it to the safety of home. Or that someone would come here and get her. Break her out. Make it easy. Out of habit, her eyes travel to the door. The robe is gone. The painting of her beautiful young self is gone. Her mother's hairbrush packed. Max's roses gone. Max is gone. She wraps her arms around herself, pulling back from the edge, willing herself not to go over.

Chapter Twenty-eight

It's after midnight when Dominic pulls the last page of the day out of the typewriter with a flourish and places it, almost reverentially, on top of the growing pile of his manuscript. The one-hundredth page of his opus. It is so satisfying to see the fruits of his labour in this decent-sized wodge of paper sitting on his desk. Productivity has suffered somewhat as a result of the visits from Roxy and Ben, but he is thoroughly enjoying having acolytes. In the last few days he has opened up more, basking in their interest and regaling them with stories of his early days. Occasionally he reads his previous day's work to them. It could be seen as self-aggrandising but there is nothing like a new and appreciative audience to make one feel wise and witty. Certainly wouldn't get that sort of approbation from Susannah, who could hardly be less interested, having made it abundantly clear that she doesn't want to hear about his book.

At some point his literary journey will end up at the Farash issue. It can't be ignored, but he has the opportunity to give it a little spin to present the correct perspective. Ideally, he'd like to open the conversation with Roxy and Ben before he commits himself on paper; get their responses to his version of events. He has a free run as long as he can keep Susannah out of it. Shouldn't be difficult – she keeps her distance when his visitors arrive, and spends most of the day in her room apart from the occasional walking of the dogs. Apparently still sulking about his little prank, she stalks past him in the house like Tragedy herself. No sense of humour. All irony is lost on her. Michelle would have seen the funny side.

Just when he could do with a little support, Susannah has become a recluse in her bedroom. Perhaps that's why Hemingway had so many wives: sooner or later they mutiny or, like Susannah, become so self-absorbed they're no help at all. Now he's forced to shop and cook for himself. After dark, Susannah emerges from her seclusion to tuck into any leftovers. She certainly won't be getting a mention in the acknowledgements – none of that *thank you to my adored wife for all your support.* He's on his own.

He toys with the idea of dedicating it to Roxy. Why not? She's his only offspring, as far as he knows. She's more interested in him and his life than anyone else, understandably. Seems to find his life fascinating and positively peppers him with questions. All the years she missed – no doubt wants to make up for lost time. He did get as far as enquiring what she does for a living and is none the wiser. Something in media sales? Neither of those words captured his imagination, let alone in combination, so he let the topic drop. Although, he should sound her out for publishing contacts. She might want to agent him. Beneath the surface charm, it's obvious she's got some steel buried in there. He admires that in a woman. She didn't get that from Michelle.

He pours himself a warming Scotch, a tonic for sleep, and a sudden thought strikes him. She hasn't mentioned it, but Roxy may already know about the Farash incident since Michelle must know about it. Roxy certainly has access to all the pieces of the puzzle, if she wanted to put them together. She may have seen it in the papers, depending on what she reads. She and Ben are chummy. Have they talked about it? Doubtful. Ben seems to have a chronic aversion to talking about other people. No reason to doubt his loyalty.

Roxy and Ben. Interesting. Perhaps it's a case of a parent being infatuated with their own progeny but Roxy seems to have twice the personality and spunk of the pensive little Mia. Roxy and Ben seem like a natural couple. They have a similar build, strong and capable looking. Roxy has a more substantial and womanly body than Mia – buxom like Michelle. Big tits and a generous backside. Likes to show it off too. None of that false modesty where women pretend to be unaware of the pleasure men derive from the glimpse of a fleshy cleavage. Michelle understood that. He thumbs through the manuscript to a description he is quietly pleased with:

I was drawn to Michelle by the dichotomies that coexisted within her character. Ethereal and maiden-like as a princess, she could rut like a peasant girl in a haystack when the occasion demanded. Beneath the ethnic bobbles and beads, beneath the sarongs and peasant skirts, she was unfettered by the constraints of undergarments. Her great round breasts, with chocolate-drop nipples, bobbed to the rhythm of her sashaying hips. Whenever she bent over, her naked buttocks were clearly visible through the taut fabric. 'Happy Valley' was open for business at any time, should the whim take us.

Life was good.

He had rather enjoyed writing this passage. Given that no one is interested in paying him to write about food or wine, perhaps he should consider a career in erotic writing, which seems to be all the go now. Or combine the two; add a new dimension to the term food porn.

On reflection, it had probably been a mistake to ditch Michelle. Things would have been near on impossible with a baby but prior to that catastrophe, their relationship had been so easy. They both had the freedom to do their own thing. Then she had to go and spoil it all. Now she's evidently happily married to a real estate agent, of all things. Michelle is a dish he wouldn't mind sampling again at this stage of his life – given the right circumstances. He wonders how happy they actually are. People probably think his union with the deranged Susannah is happy. The truth will eventually prevail. His readers will see how selfless he has been in sticking by her thus far.

He refills his glass, switches off the desk lamp and lights a cigar. Through the window rain falls steadily, the dying fire refracting splinters of light on the glass. He turns his full attention to the flavour profile of the cigar, breathing and tasting it simultaneously, coaxing every possible nuance from it. It's a cunning little devil, starting with a smooth caramel flavour, then in the next breath a touch of saltiness followed by a more provocative hint of spice: mustardy, with a suggestion of cumin. It continues to intrigue, revealing layers of flavour that lead him to wonder if perhaps the hiatus between decent meals has to some degree restored his taste receptors. It's possible that his papillae are regenerating and, at this point, even the slightest improvement would be welcome.

He is slowly eking out his last bottle of thirty-year-old Scotch, savouring every resonant sip as it adds a toffee sweetness to the cigar flavour. The cigar, the whisky, the quiet ambience of the room, his one-hundred-page achievement and the titillating memories of Michelle's glorious breasts combine to produce a surprising feeling of wellbeing. He even feels a tiny stirring in the loins that indicates some resurgence of his long-lost libido.

Chapter Twenty-nine

Ben's not sure whether he felt obliged to invite Roxy over, or genuinely wanted her to see the house. Maybe a bit of both. He feels sorry for her. She seems lost, sitting around having to wait for an invite from Dominic and not really having anything else to do but hang around her hotel. Most of the old village is closed for winter. And now, after a couple of sunny days, the weather has turned to rain again.

Even with the heating on in their workrooms, both he and Mia wear coats all day. The combination of the cold and damp makes him feel miserable and depressed. Now his work is on pause until early January and he's been trying to muster some enthusiasm for his own development projects but finds himself regularly standing at the window, hands in pockets, staring out across the fields at the bleak misty landscape.

When Roxy arrives, she gets a tour of the house that finishes in the kitchen, which is warm and pleasant with the lingering smell of baking, Mia having knocked up some little cakes for the occasion. Once the introductions are done,

Mia puts the coffee and cakes out on the table and they all sit down.

Roxy looks around the kitchen, soaking it all up. 'You two are living the life, aren't you? This house is like something out of a movie. I'd love to do what you're doing – if I could get myself together and escape from London. I wouldn't do it on my own, obviously. That'd be tough.'

Ben can't help but feel he and Mia are a couple of fakers, their 'dream life' a facade with nothing of substance behind it. And, despite Roxy's enthusiasm, Ben can tell that Mia doesn't like her. She's watchful and reserved, glancing at him to see his reactions.

'Living here is not as easy as it looks,' says Mia. 'Takes a bit of getting used to. It's harder than we thought, anyway.'

'Especially in winter, I imagine. It's early days for you, I suppose. Susannah and Dominic seem to have settled in. They obviously love it here.'

Mia says nothing but Ben feels duty-bound to confirm the Harringtons' satisfaction.

'Considering they didn't necessarily want to come and live in France,' adds Roxy.

'Then why did they?' asks Mia.

'Oh, you don't know? I thought it was all out in the open,' says Roxy.

'If it is, we don't know about it.' Mia looks across at Ben. 'Or, I don't, anyway.'

'Well, you know he was a food critic. He was a bit of a celeb back in the day. He was a good-looking guy, friends in all the right places. What happened was that he gave a restaurant a bad review and the owner, a guy called Farash, did himself in. So the press came after Dominic.'

Ben feels almost relieved. It could have been something much worse. 'That's hardly his fault. He couldn't have known the outcome.'

'So he's never talked to you about it?' asks Roxy.

'Never,' confirms Ben. 'I don't think it's any of our business. They obviously came here to get away from all that. It must have been horrible for Dominic.'

'Do they know that's definitely the reason the man . . .?' asks Mia. 'He might have had other things going on.'

'Apparently the restaurant went downhill pretty quickly,' says Roxy. 'It happened the same week the restaurant closed down.'

'Must have been a very harsh review,' says Mia. 'To have that effect.'

'But if Dominic had a bad experience, then it was his job to write about it,' insists Ben.

'He's a funny guy, isn't he?' says Roxy. 'He's like the lord of the manor sometimes. Like he thinks we're his subjects, come to kneel at his feet.'

'What did he call us the other day?'

'Acolytes!' Roxy laughs.

'What the hell?' Ben does a quick search on his phone and reads out: 'An assistant or helper. Minion . . . Lackey. What?!'

Mia watches them laughing. Ben wonders why she doesn't get Dominic. She takes everything he says seriously when it is so obviously meant to get a reaction.

'You don't mind him referring to you as his lackey?' asks Mia.

Roxy brushes away tears of laughter. 'Not at all. I don't take it personally. That's part of his style. His biting wit.'

'Maybe,' says Mia. 'I certainly wouldn't want to be one of his acolytes and I wouldn't want to get on the wrong side of him, either.'

'Hold on, you're talking about Roxy's dad, Mia,' cautions Ben.

'Oh, don't worry, I get what you're saying but I think he's a pussycat, don't you, Ben?' Roxy turns to him for confirmation.

Ben doesn't want to ostracise Mia further, just bring her into the fold. 'He's really not as bad as you think. You're being oversensitive, Mia-Cat.'

His endearment does nothing to ease the tension in the room. Mia's gaze is on Roxy. 'Why did you choose now to come and find him? Why not last year or five years ago?' she asks.

Roxy shrugs. 'Ben and I have talked about that too.'

Ben feels Mia's eyes slowly shift to him as though he has already betrayed her in some way.

'I can't seem to decide what I want to do with my life,' continues Roxy, unaware the atmosphere is freezing over. 'My last relationship was a disaster. I thought it was time to regroup. Figure out who I am. Michelle always told me that Dominic wouldn't be interested. That he'd never once been to see me, even in the hospital when I was born. So I decided to find out for myself.'

It seems to Ben that it's kind of heroic to turn up and take your chances, to risk that sort of rejection a second time. Mia can't seem to get that Roxy is trying to be friendly and open with her.

Ben walks Roxy to the door and stands on the front step as she drives away. She knows more than she's saying, he can tell, but he doesn't want to hear it. He doesn't want to be burdened with information he didn't want in the first place. It's an uncomfortable feeling that takes him back to when he was a kid and he'd overhear his mother laughing softly into the phone. 'I have to go,' she'd say. He'd ask her who she was talking to and she'd name this friend or that but she never laughed in that secretive way with her friends. Her voice was thick with the unspoken. He came home from school early one Friday, the day his father always went into town. He stood in the kitchen and watched his mother hurrying across the paddock. She walked in humming to herself and almost collapsed at the sight of him standing there. He was older then. He noticed the buttons on her shirt were done up wrong. He never even told Ollie. He loved his mother, she was gentle and kind, but he felt from that day that she was lost to them. She had another life. A private life. And he felt burdened by the knowledge. After that he noticed how she stared out the window, across the paddocks, wishing she was over there instead of with them. It hurt to see her do that and he wished he didn't know why.

Now he is faced with this information that isn't their business. If he had to hear about it, he would have preferred it come from Dominic, so that at least he knew it was accurate. Now he has to pretend not to know when Dominic eventually tells him.

Mia cleans up the kitchen in an angry banging way. Ben stands in the doorway, taking in her pinched silence. 'I don't know what's wrong with you, but that was really rude,' he says.

'That was the best I could do,' she says without looking up.

'I thought we were going to make new friends here. You seem to be determined to alienate everyone. Where's that going to get us?'

Mia stops work and looks at him. 'You know what? I don't really believe her. I don't trust her, the same way I don't trust *him*. And both of them seem to have sucked you in somehow. You're *her* lackey too. Running around after her —'

'I'm not "sucked in", and the whole lackey thing was a joke. Joke? And to be honest, you're really starting to annoy the crap out of me. I came here for you —'

'I knew we'd get to this at some point.'

'Yeah, well, I think we're at that point now.'

Mia stares back at him, meeting his hostility with her own. 'So what comes after that point?'

Ben turns away from her. He doesn't know. He doesn't have a clue what comes after that point.

Chapter Thirty

I know this is temporary. I know that Ben and I will find our way out somehow, but right now it feels like we're strangers trapped in this alternate universe. Everything we shared three months ago seems to have dissolved. He's like another person. Someone shut off to me. I imagine him opening up that spreadsheet, his finger hovering over the delete button, scrolling down the list of all those things he loves about me. He goes out nearly every day without inviting me or even telling me where he's going. That's so not like him.

This morning Chloe and Madame Bellamy are visiting. I'm not really in the mood after the conversation with Ben yesterday but it's a good distraction. I've baked a *quatre-quarts*, otherwise known as a pound cake, with swirls of chocolate through it.

I lay out our morning tea with some of Madame Levant's cups and plates on the big table in the summer room, and we sit down together at one end. Gentle rain drizzles down the windows. The room is filled with silver light.

Madame Bellamy looks over the boxes I have opened and notices the books on the shelves. 'You like books?' she asks. 'French books?'

'I've read some Colette and Flaubert, and plan to read all these.'

'Your French is very good,' she says with a smile. 'And your baking is excellent too.' She tilts her cup in tribute. 'It was me who put these boxes away upstairs; everything had to be cleared for the sale. Madame had many lovely things, so I put some aside for the new owners. I'm pleased you will keep them.'

'Mia's an artist too, *Maman*,' adds Chloe, as though this is a job interview.

I show her some of the drawings I've been working on. Mainly sketches of furnishings and features of the house: the staircase, the French doors in this room, the front gates and the goats. Madame Bellamy looks them over carefully, one by one. She looks closely at the drawing of Esmée's little bed with the canopy draped over it.

'You have a special interest in Esmée,' she says, looking up at me. 'Why?'

I don't understand myself, so decide to be honest. 'I have a sense of her being here in the house. I went to the cemetery to find out about her . . . I have dreams about her . . .'

She looks around the room and out into the rainy afternoon, saying nothing.

'Perhaps this is not the right time,' says Chloe, touching her mother's arm.

'I'm interested in the family and the history too,' I say, hoping to encourage her.

'I can tell you about the family; we can start there,' she says. 'Madame Levant and my mother grew up together, our families were friends. To me she was always tante Mathilde. As a young woman, Mathilde would design and make beautiful clothes, both for herself and for my mother. She was very talented but also ambitious. After the liberation of France, Mathilde went to live in Paris, against her parents' will. Her only brother was killed late in the war, so they wanted their daughter at home. It was unusual then for a young woman of only twenty to leave this village to work in Paris, which many people here, even today, believe . . . Let's just say that we don't regard the city with the same romantic sentimentality that foreigners do!' She smiles.

'Mathilde lived with an aunt who helped her find work with a *couturier*. The time after the liberation was exciting; French haute couture blossomed out of the ruins of Paris. Even in her last years, when she was not well, tante Mathilde often talked about this time when the eyes of the world were on France and the style of French women, and our nation could lift its head high again.

'In 1946 she was approached by a *couturier* who was opening his own salon and looking for staff. He had seen her work and offered her a position in his workroom as a *première* – a very prestigious appointment, especially for such a young woman. She liked this *couturier*, he was shy and polite, and extremely talented.

'In spring of the next year the salon showed their first collection – it was an immediate success and everything took off at great speed. Mathilde became engaged to be married to a young man called Hugo, but she kept delaying the wedding because of the demands of her work.

'Perhaps she didn't really want to be married, although she never said this, but I think if you are madly in love, you can't wait to share your life with your lover, no? They eventually married sometime in 1949 and Esmée was born one year later, the same year that I was born. Our mothers were still close and overjoyed to have daughters the same age.

'At that time it was more difficult for women to work once they were married, especially if they had children, but the *couturier*, whom they called *le patron*, was sympathetic towards women and he didn't want to lose Mathilde. The couture business was growing rapidly and she was under a lot of pressure, but she loved the work and didn't want to leave.

'The Levants came here often to stay with Esmée's grandparents. She was like a cousin to me and, when they visited, we would play together every day.

'At the time I was to start *cours préparatoire*, at age six, there was a problem between the Levants and they separated. Mathilde brought Esmée here to live with her grandparents for a while, perhaps while she decided what to do. So, then Esmée and I went to the school just up the road together, and we became like sisters.'

Madame Bellamy pauses. She gets up from the table and walks over to the windows. She stands looking out into the gloomy afternoon, gathering her thoughts.

'You don't have to talk about it, *Maman*,' Chloe tells her. 'Mia will understand.'

'Of course, you don't need to explain anything to me,' I assure her.

'It's a long time ago,' she says, turning towards us, her expression troubled. 'But I feel you have an affinity, and you deserve to hear this story. I know you will take care of it.'

She sits down at the table again and begins. 'We would walk home together every day. It wasn't far and in those days children wandered everywhere without supervision. It had been raining for days. People said Le Cérou would flood soon and we decided to go to Pont Saint-Pierre to see for ourselves. The sides of the bridge are low and the water was higher than we had ever seen it and beginning to flood over the banks. We gathered sticks and played a game of throwing them over one side then rushing to the other side to see whose stick had won – all children love this game.

'I was waiting for my stick to appear and I turned back but Esmée had gone. I looked around . . . then I saw her . . . it was terrible . . . terrible . . . her yellow raincoat, hair flowing as she was swept along, twisting and turning in the water as though she had become part of the river.'

Chloe's eyes are bright with tears, but Madame Bellamy seems determined to push on with her story. 'I ran to the nearest house and told Monsieur Martin and he ran straight down to the river. I was crying and frightened but I had no experience of death and I didn't understand how serious it was. Someone came to help me. I remember so many people coming out in the rain to search. My mother was there, holding me; we were crying together. I was so ashamed we had caused all this trouble. They looked for Esmée for hours. It was night when they found her.'

Madame Bellamy is silent for a moment, her eyes darkened by memories. I feel as though my heart is breaking for little Esmée and for her friend, still hurting all these years later, whose life could never be the same.

'As you know, Le Cérou is not a big river, it's small and gentle,' continues Madame Bellamy quietly. 'We would often play there or have picnics in the summer. We didn't understand that it had changed that day and become dangerous. We were just little children.'

'Tante Mathilde came home that night. I remember everyone crying and distraught. It was a terrible time. After that, Mathilde left her job and the life she had built in Paris and she came home to Cordes. She told me in her last years that she had lost heart; it didn't mean anything to her any more. But I think she was also punishing herself. For not being a better mother, for not being here to take care of Esmée.'

'But even if she had been here, you would have walked home from school just the same, it wouldn't have made a difference,' says Chloe. 'I pick Alain and Felix up sometimes but most days they walk home, just as all the other children do.'

'Of course, this is logical but grief is not logical. She couldn't forgive herself. It's natural to think that you could have done something different and changed history. But how can we ever know that tragedy is about to strike? I have forgiven myself, I think. I was only six years old. There was nothing I could do. But it was a terrible tragedy and it broke my mother's heart too. It has made me very cautious in my life, knowing what can happen.

'So this is why I looked after tante Mathilde in the last few years since she became unwell. I cared for her as a daughter and that has helped me bring our history together to a close.'

I thank her for telling me her story – it means more to me than she could know.

'I wanted you to know because I sense some tragedy in your own life,' she says. 'And I want to tell you that, in her last years, Mathilde regretted her course of action. She didn't have the strength to go on but she felt that, had she continued the work she loved, it would have offered her a solace. She regretted that she wasn't able to accept this was the blow that life had dealt her. She gave up her dreams. It was only later she realised that this sacrifice was pointless.'

'Perhaps you should explain about the house too, *Maman*,' says Chloe.

'Of course. This is not known in the village because I don't want people to think the wrong thing. So this is our secret. I was the only beneficiary of Madame Levant's will. The house was left to me on the condition that it was sold. It was she who stipulated a young couple, not me. I can see you have respect for the house and the history and there are many stories – happier ones – that I will share with you in time. But this was the important one.'

Later, as we say goodbye at the front door, she says, 'You probably know that locals call this house *la villa jonquille* – this is not because of its colour, as you will discover in the spring – if you find a new home for the goats. Every winter since Esmée's death, Mathilde planted a basketful of daffodils in her memory. I put the goats in here to frighten away vandals, but they eat the flowers, and so there have not been any daffodils these last years.'

I assure her that we will make sure the daffodils have a chance to flower and she must come and see the blooms. It's only when they've gone that I realise it's unlikely we'll still be here when spring comes.

Two days before Christmas, I arrive home from my afternoon walk to find Susannah sitting in her car parked outside our house. When I reach the car, she doesn't get out but leans over and opens the passenger door. I slide into the seat and close the door.

'Sorry to do this, I'm not meaning to act like some sort of secret agent . . . it's just . . .'

'Would you like to come inside for a cup of tea, Susannah?'

'Thank you, but I wanted to make sure we weren't overheard. I'm sorry, I know you didn't ever want to be involved with this. I have four more bottles to sell, then that's it, I won't ever bother you again.'

'Susannah, I do want to help you, I can see it's difficult for you . . . but . . .'

'I'm leaving him.' She stares out the windscreen, her eyes wide with shock, as if someone else just made this statement. She turns to me, her eyes bright with tears. 'I'm so frightened.' She grabs my hand and squeezes it. 'You can't imagine how frightening it is.'

'Oh, Susannah, I can imagine. I have been through it. Ben and I split up six months ago and then got back together.'

She stares at me in disbelief. 'How is that possible? You two are made for each other.'

'My fault completely. I didn't deal with the fact that we couldn't have children.'

'It can never be completely the fault of one person. Now you're the one being hard on yourself. I would have liked children too. My first husband Max would have liked them, but I wasn't ready. Then when I was ready, Dominic wouldn't hear of it.' She releases my hand. 'I'm not sure I should confess this, it seems so weak . . . but I had three terminations. I could say Dominic made me but you can't make someone do that. I was afraid that I couldn't do it on my own. People say you shouldn't look back, no regrets and all that . . . I have nothing but regrets. That's why I have to leave now . . . even though I'm so terrified.'

'You will be fine. It's obviously going to be hard at first . . .'

'My husband, my first husband, Max, was going to help me . . .' She collapses in tears. 'He *died*. He just died last week. I can't believe it. I didn't have a chance to see him or tell him the things I should have . . . I never told him how wretched I feel for what I did to him!' She leans her forehead on the steering wheel. 'I feel like a rickety old boat covered with these . . . barnacles . . . of regret . . . weighing me down, dragging me deeper and deeper . . .' She lifts her head and stares at me. 'If I don't do something soon, I'll disappear below the surface forever.'

There's nothing I can say that will make this any easier for Susannah. I offer the usual reassurances and my support. She just nods her head numbly and hands me the bag with the last bottles to sell. As I get out of the car, she clutches my arm. 'Mia, I probably won't have a chance to say a proper goodbye to you, so I'll say it now. I can't thank you enough for everything you've done for me. I wouldn't be able to leave if you hadn't helped me, you know. I'll never forget.'

As I walk through the gates, across the gravel entry and up the front steps, I'm gripped with the most terrible sense of foreboding that this will not go well.

Christmas Eve, and Ben's disappeared again this evening. As usual, he didn't tell me where he was going, which probably means he's over at Dominic's and doesn't think I would approve. He's right, I don't approve. But I'm not his mother, so have no jurisdiction over him. I thought when his work closed down over Christmas, we'd start on one of the projects in our book, but he's not keen. He said he needs a break.

I would have liked to go up to the village this evening, maybe even to Mass, although we're not Catholics. Tonight is the French Christmas but in our house, it's just like every other night and here I am sitting at the kitchen table eating eggs on toast for dinner.

The meringue base for tomorrow's pavlova is baking slowly in the oven. I message Ollie to find out if she can video chat; she comes straight back saying she's available in ten minutes. I get out my pad and start to doodle, drawing shapes and patterns and letting them build and change and evolve and they start to turn into the familiar faces of the pugs. My mind wanders, hearing only the sound of the soft pencil on paper, my hand engaged, my brain effortlessly following and building lines and curves as they come to life on the page. Lost in the moment, I leap at the sound of the call coming through and hit the button.

'*Bonjour! Ça va?*' Ollie grins. 'How's it going, *mon amie?*'

The sight of her face puts a smile on mine. 'Fine, all good —'

'I'll get the kids, they've been up since dawn. Santa's done a great job. Where's Ben?'

'He's not here. I don't know where he is.'

Her smile fades. 'What's going on, Madame Tinker?'

'We've made the most horrible mistake coming here,' I hear myself say. 'I don't even know what we were thinking. How it could possibly work . . .'

'Hang on, hang on – even a month ago it was all happy days, you were having a wonderful time. This is probably just a blip, you can't expect everything to go perfectly the whole time. It's going to be hard at some point, it's not like the movies.'

'Are you saying there's no happy ending?' I ask. 'That's depressing.'

'Nothing's guaranteed. I haven't heard from Ben in ages. What's happening with him?'

'Right now, he's always either on his computer or he's out with his friends.'

'Ben has friends? That's surprising, and they're not your friends?'

I give her a background briefing on Dominic and Susannah, and the situation with the wine, and finally Roxy and where she fits in, although that's still something of a mystery to me.

'So have you done a search on any of these people to find out more?'

'I don't really have enough details. I don't know the Harringtons' real name. I don't actually know Roxy's surname. Ben probably does but you know what he's like, he's not going to be poking around online spying on people.'

'Plus, I guess, the more you find out, the more you have to keep from Ben.'

'Exactly, otherwise it looks like I'm building a case against them. I don't know what to do. I feel as though we need to get away, just the two of us, but there's so much to be done here, he won't agree to that. And, the worst part? We're having Christmas with them.'

'Jesus, it's like the plot of one of those terrible American movies where everything goes wrong on Christmas Day. Maybe Dominic will get zapped by the fairy lights, although sounds as though he'd need something more high voltage to kill him. Okay, here's a plan —'

'Yeah, thanks, Ol. I don't want to end up in a French prison for the rest of my natural life.'

'Not an assassination plan, you nutcase. I'm going to suggest to Ben that you guys take some time and have a few days in Paris, and regroup, romantically speaking. What do you reckon?'

'It's worth a try. Anything is worth a try. I really just want to come home. I never should have agreed to this,' I say in a wobbly voice. 'I want to be warm. And be with my friends. And never have to see the Harringtons or that creepy Roxy ever again. I can't even tell you how much I dislike her. She's such a . . . frigging . . . skank . . .'

Ollie's expression morphs to one of wide-eyed horror, and I spin around to see Roxy and Ben standing in the doorway.

Chapter Thirty-one

Christmas Eve brings thunderous skies and misty rain. Susannah surveys her bedroom, now in that indefinable state between chaos and organisation. All the preparations for her last hurrah tomorrow and the emotions stirred up by the packing have left her feeling wrung out. She is both determined to leave on Boxing Day and ambivalent at the same time. It doesn't absolutely *have* to be Boxing Day, but she should definitely start the new year back home.

The thought of living with Reggie is not terribly attractive. Although he's quite good company, and his little mews house is convenient, she and Becky have always shared jokes about him being 'Reggie-mented'. Every day scheduled from start to end. Each day of the week has a dedicated meal that his housekeeper, Mrs Hemming, prepares in the afternoon before going home. He holds a firm belief in the power of the microwave to neutralise bacteria and reheats his meals until they blister and pop like molten lava. On Fridays he dines at the club, always at the same table, like the last remnant of a previous generation.

Susannah will be expected to fit in with his schedule, without delays or disruption. If her mother were still alive, his life would be so completely different. All of their lives would be different. Susannah was only ten years old when she died and remembers her mother only as lively and fun. Her father was the strict and frugal one. He was the sobering influence. It was only after her mother's death that he softened and became more indulgent. Perhaps he regretted not revealing that side of himself earlier. He has been a good father and Susannah determines to do her best to not create disturbance around him. Her greatest fear is that Dominic could turn up and scenes erupt. Reggie will not tolerate that for one minute.

Once she has found some sort of work, she plans to use the money she has tucked away from her ill-gotten gains and rent a little place. She envisages a quiet little flat where the morning sun spills through the windows; a bowl of pink roses glow on a polished table. Perhaps there'd be pleasant neighbours who would invite her in for a drink or a meal occasionally. She will, she decides, be grateful for any sort of work, perhaps not cleaning or house-keeping, but she can see herself in a tasteful little shop somewhere, or perhaps a department store, wearing make-up and nice clothes. There is reason for optimism. That's where her focus needs to be, holding tight to the lucky charm of her bright sparkly future.

Downstairs the house is finally in order in a way that it hasn't been for some time. His nibs has been in his study most of the day, oblivious to the industry outside his sanctuary. She opens his door and stands watching him tapping away at his typewriter. Look at you, she thinks. How many stinging insults I have toler-ated over the last few years about my 'faded glory' and 'decrepit old age'. And you, oblivious to the belly that strains against your jumper, your broken capillaries, sagging jowls and hairy nostrils. When you look in the mirror, you must magically see the man you once were. You're pretty decrepit yourself, Mister.

'Is there a reason you're lingering wistfully at the door?' Dominic asks without looking up. 'Perhaps rethinking your strategy? Should I prepare myself to gracefully accept a heartfelt apology from you, or get my riot gear on?'

'I'm going outside to bring some more wood up for the fire. I can bring up the wine for lunch tomorrow if you like.'

He has a hearty fire burning in the grate, which explains where the logs for the living-room fire disappeared to. He ignores her, continuing to type, steadily tap-tapping at that antiquated typewriter.

'Dominic, I really think we should declare a truce. Otherwise we're not going to get through Christmas Day without an embarrassing incident.'

'You're negotiating a truce now?' He looks up in mock surprise. 'I wasn't aware there had been a declaration of war. What I experienced was a pre-emptive strike that's left me with possibly permanent injury. Perhaps you're aware that there are protocols, the Geneva Convention, for example?'

'Please, don't try to rile me. You've had your revenge. Can we agree on a truce, just for the next few days? It's freezing outside, I've got my coat on and I'm offering to go to the cellar for you.'

'Yes, I see that. And I'm wondering what you're really up to, you little minx.' His tone is both mocking and hostile.

Susannah forces a smile. 'Just trying to be helpful, dear. I don't want to live in a state of siege any more than you do.'

He seems to buy it and writes down his instructions to bring up four wines, giving her the exact locations among the numbered racks. 'You know where the key is, don't you?' he adds, going back to his work. Of course she does.

She's so relieved, she practically runs from the room. As she steps outside, an icy wind whips at her face. The pugs resist coming out and then, in desperation, charge out for a pee and hurry straight back inside to their cushion by the radiator, now on low in preparation for tomorrow. As she closes the door behind them, she notices that Dominic has had his nasty little chainsaw out and her yard broom now lies in a dozen pieces.

Chapter Thirty-two

Ben catches Roxy as she runs down the front steps, grabbing her arm. 'Look, I'm sorry,' he says. 'I'm really sorry. That was so embarrassing. I don't know what to say.'

'Forget it. I never should have come here. Susannah hates me. Mia hates me.' She pulls away from him and walks quickly back to her car.

Not knowing what to do, Ben keeps pace with her. 'I don't think you should drive like this, you're upset. And you've been drinking.'

'I'll be fine!' She opens the door angrily. 'Go away, go inside.'

Ben holds out his hand. 'Give me the key, I'll drive you up the hill and walk home.'

'Don't be ridiculous! You don't need to do that.'

Ben peels her fingers open and removes the key from her grip. He leads her around to the passenger door and opens it. Calming upset women is something he does well. She obediently gets in and puts on her seatbelt. They are both silent as he drives up the hill to the village.

Ben has always understood that his loyalties lie one hundred per cent with Mia. He would back her against his mother, even against Ollie if it absolutely came to it, because that was the terms of his contract. However, he's less and less certain about the contract and its validity. He and Mia hardly see eye-to-eye on anything; right now it's hard to imagine what they have in common and how and when that changed. He wonders if their separation, and her hooking up with that lame-arse Isaac, has caused a permanent scar that will never truly heal.

It's a struggle to get his thoughts straight and work out what to do. It was beyond embarrassing to walk in and hear Mia bagging out not just Dominic and Susannah but Roxy as well. Skank? He'd never heard Mia talk about someone like that before.

He'd got a lift back from the Harringtons' with Roxy and had invited her in for a cup of tea, hoping that Mia would still be up. Maybe the two of them would be more relaxed and it would make things easier for Christmas lunch tomorrow. Mia making Roxy her enemy was doing his head in. According to Roxy, Susannah seems to want nothing to do with her either. Susannah avoids him as well but she isn't his stepmother, so not such a big deal.

When she realised that Ben and Roxy were there, Mia tried to pretend nothing had happened. Ollie just bailed and quit the call. Easy for her.

Ben parks Roxy's car in the ramparts parking area. He switches off the ignition and hands her the key. When she takes it from him and wraps her hand around his, he knows he's in trouble. When she leans over and presses her lips to his, he has a sense of being cut loose from his life, like an astronaut floating helplessly in space. The soft warmth of her mouth on his, a faint smell of citrus perfume on her skin. They kiss as though both knew this moment was coming, it just needed to find its tipping point and over they go. She slips her hands inside his jacket and tugs at his shirt. 'Come up to my room,' she whispers.

He gets out of the car as if in a dream. He allows her to take his hand and lead him towards her hotel. The front door is locked at night and, as she fumbles in her handbag for the key, he feels a wave of nausea as though his gut is being compressed, his mouth instantly awash with saliva. He turns away and rushes down a side path until he finds a piece of garden where he heaves up the contents of his stomach. He leans his burning cheek against the wet stone wall and wipes his mouth on his sleeve.

Roxy appears, walking down the path towards him. 'Found it. Come on. Are you okay?'

'Yeah, fine. Sorry. I don't know what I'm doing,' he says. 'I need to go home. See you tomorrow.'

He walks all the way home in the dark, a light rain falling, his jacket nowhere near warm enough for the damp cold of the night. He tries to think his normal rational ordered thoughts about what happened this evening but it's all so tangled and upsetting that he wonders if he drank more than he realised. He must have been pissed to let his guard down like that. To compromise everything, absolutely everything, for someone he barely knows. One thing is certain, he's not himself. He doesn't even know who he's become. How did he not know how difficult this whole thing would be? It seemed like such an unbelievable adventure. All their friends were so envious. He didn't think it through and sees now that it's absolutely doomed to failure.

As he walks, it dawns on him that he's done exactly what his mother did. She was unhappy and she found an escape route; led a double life. He remembers her expression that afternoon when she walked in the door, before she realised he was home. She looked flushed and alive, almost carefree, like a younger version of herself. That is not how he feels right now. He feels like shit. Like an idiot. He doesn't know what he's going to say to Mia. All he wants to do right now is get straight on his computer and book his ticket home. Make a run for it.

Chapter Thirty-three

As soon as Ben gets into bed, I can smell that woman on him. She wears a perfume that smells like lemon detergent. She must have been pretty close for it to rub off. I've never been here before, never had a moment's mistrust of Ben. I don't know what to do or what to say without making things worse. I can't even work out if I want to know what has happened between them or pretend I don't notice. Knowing could be worse than not knowing.

I don't speak and neither does he. I don't sleep and neither does he. We both lie quietly, breathing and saying nothing. Sometime in the early hours of the morning I ask, 'What's happening?'

'I don't know,' he says.

'Are we finished?'

There's the longest silence and finally he says in a sad voice, 'I don't know.'

That's not Ben. Never has he doubted. I'm the doubter, the mercurial one. I'm the one who needs talking down off life's ledges. I rely on his solidness, his commitment, his belief in us. Ben is the constant in my life.

'Did you sleep with her?' I ask the darkness.

'No,' he says.

Ben wouldn't lie but he might use a technicality.

'I can't talk to you while you smell of her.'

'Who says I want to talk? It's two in the morning. Go to sleep.'

'Do you want to go home?'

He thinks about this for a while and says, 'It's not what I thought it would be. It's not working. And it's not going to work.'

'You haven't given it a chance,' I say, wide awake now.

He gives a groan and half sits up, pulling his pillow up behind him. 'Okay, we have to talk now, do we? Everything can't be your way all the time, Mia. This is too hard, there's nothing in it for me. I thought I'd be fine with it, but I'm not.'

'And, if I want to stay?'

'That's up to you,' he says. 'You make your own decision.'

'You don't love me any more.'

'Mia, it's got nothing to do with that. That doesn't change. It's just stupid asking me that. Like blackmail: "if you love me you'll do what I want".'

'Is there something going on with Roxy?'

'She kissed me is all that happened.'

'Did you want her to? Did you kiss her back?'

'Look, it's something that happened. I walked into it, but then I walked away and that's what matters. And I'm not going back. I'm just completely lost. I don't know where to turn.'

In that moment I understand that it's down to me to try to make this work. I want to tell him to turn to me, but I'm afraid that it won't be enough to make him stay and I am silent.

Chapter Thirty-four

The boiler has done its work overnight, and the house is pleasantly warm. Susannah has set the kindling ready to light the living-room fire an hour before the guests arrive. The kitchen is clean and organised. The vegetables are prepared and *hors d'oeuvres* artfully arranged and soon the smell of roasting turkey will waft from the oven. She has surpassed herself.

When the Tinkers arrive, their faces pinched with cold, both seem beset by some unnameable misery. They are usually so sweet and dewy, like the proverbial breath of fresh air cutting through the stagnant disappointment of the Harrington household. Not today. Both look wretched. Ben undertakes to coax Dominic out of his study. Mia follows Susannah into the kitchen with the pavlova she has semi-prepared for dessert.

As soon as they are alone, Mia says quietly, 'Everything has sold.' She holds up her phone to show Susannah the statement. Susannah puts on her glasses and takes the phone, frowning at the screen. It's far more than she anticipated and she feels a rush of self-recrimination. She hadn't known herself capable of such crimes. She's been taking bottles randomly but when Mia told her the going rate for the Romanée-Conti, she knew they were out on a very dangerous limb. She attempts to extinguish her guilt with a blast of furious indignation. With all their money problems, despite all her tears and entreaties, Dominic has not once suggested selling any of these wines worth thousands – tens of thousands!

'Well, that's it, it's finished. Thank you so much,' says Susannah, handing the phone back.

'What are you two whispering about?' Roxy says, walking in. 'Like a couple of schoolgirls!'

Mia says nothing and turns away, ignoring her.

'Just planning lunch,' Susannah says. Opening the fridge, she lifts out the tray of *hors d'oeuvres* and hands it to Roxy. 'Perhaps you'd like to put these on the coffee table and remind Dominic to get everyone drinks.'

When she's sure Roxy is out of earshot, Susannah whispers, 'I brought the wine up for today, so it could be weeks before he finds out. Hopefully, I'll be safely out of the way by then.'

She and Mia join the others in the living room. Dominic has emerged to play host and bask in compliments for the splendid fire, flower arrangements and festive decorations. They're going to play happy families today. Susannah feels a bitter satisfaction that he has unwittingly financed these fripperies and shown no curiosity whatsoever as to how they were purchased. He takes for granted that they still have electricity.

On the surface, this scene is exactly what Susannah had hoped for when the Tinkers first arrived. And yet the reality is impossibly distant from her imaginings. Apart from the undercurrent with Dominic, Roxy strikes a discordant note and emits a strange confidence. That same sense of entitlement that Dominic possesses. There's a smugness about her, as though she's nursing a secret.

Champagne is poured, toasts made – to France! *La bonne vie!* Friends! Family! – accompanied by a local *foie gras* on triangles of toast. They had agreed not to exchange gifts, but Mia gives her a beautiful drawing of Lou and Chou rendered in pencil and ink that almost undoes Susannah in her highly strung state.

'Enchanting,' remarks Dominic. 'Which is which?'

'It's very obvious. Lou's little teardrop. Chou's almond eyes. You've captured them so beautifully, Mia. Thank you,' says Susannah, giving her a kiss.

'Yes, well, let's not get bogged down in argument when these folks are barely in the door,' says Dominic. 'Sit down, sit down – more champagne!'

If drama school taught Susannah anything, it was the nuances of body language. When Roxy sits down next to Ben, there's an unmistakeable sense of intimacy. Mia sits apart. She looks pale and peaky and Ben is very subdued. Dear God, what has this ghastly woman done to divide this beautiful young couple?

Susannah is gripped by a sense of premonition that something will go horribly wrong today. As soon as she deems it acceptable, she busies herself with lunch, ignoring Dominic's protestations at her haste, insisting the turkey with its chestnut stuffing will dry out. From the kitchen, she can hear the distant sound of the telephone ringing in her room above. It almost never rings but it's probably Becky. She will call her back later and firm up the arrangements for her arrival.

They move into the dining room and take their places. The table does look divine with the silver candelabras – which took forever to polish – her best silver, the crystal wine glasses and the gold-and-white dinner set. Flowers and napkins are all in green and red.

Dashing between the kitchen and dining room, Susannah notices that Roxy's phone, left on a side table, gives a slight buzzing and the screen lights up. Then it stops and starts again. With a quick look over her shoulder, Susannah picks it up. It stops buzzing and shows six missed calls, all from Michelle. Roxy often refers to her mother as Michelle, in fact 'Mum' sounds a little forced on the odd occasion when she uses it.

Once all the serving dishes are on the table, Susannah sits down and Dominic opens the wine he has chosen for the main course, a Languedoc red – and proceeds to give their guests an unnecessary lesson in wine appreciation. He raises his glass to propose yet another toast. 'I'd like to offer a salutation to myself, actually. This morning I completed the writing of my memoir.'

Susannah realises with a jolt that he won't be confining himself to his study now, which will make her escape a little more complicated. 'Surely that's just the first draft, Dominic? You can't have finished it already?'

'I write carefully, Susannah,' he says, enunciating each word.

They all raise their glasses, even though Roxy is the only one who seems to genuinely share his enthusiasm. 'I can't wait to read it! Congratulations!' she says.

'And so you shall,' says Dominic. 'You might like to take it back with you when you go, and have it copied for me while I decide where to send it. Guard it with your life, obviously.'

'You must be excited to read it, Susannah?' asks Roxy.

'I wouldn't say excited. I don't know what he's said about me. And I'm not sure I want to know.'

'Ahhh,' says Dominic. 'Once a prima donna, always a prima donna. Perhaps the success of my book could pave the way for that elusive acting career you've been pining after for the last couple of decades. Then you'd be pleased, wouldn't you? Put you back in that spotlight that you crave so much.'

'Okay, Dominic . . .' Susannah begins. 'Let's not go there —'

'It's something of a misnomer that Susannah even identifies as an "actress". It's really for want of being able to identify as anything else. She's a pampered pooch who was put through the best acting school in London by her slightly daft daddy, and given a couple of stage roles at the behest of her even more indulgent former husband who has been hovering over her ever since like her fussy old guardian angel.'

'You're very cruel sometimes, Dominic,' says Mia. 'That's really not nice. Susannah doesn't deserve that.'

Ben looks at Susannah as though wondering if this is normal banter. No one knows how to stop Dominic and Roxy doesn't want him to stop. She practically crackles with interest, her gaze bright and attentive.

Susannah burns with humiliation. 'You are cruel. And that's not true.' She hasn't even told Dominic that Maxwell is gone. She doesn't want to have that conversation; it's not as though he would offer any comfort. More likely he'd crow about his ability to outlive Maxwell.

'Oh, for goodness sake, don't take it all so seriously. Have some more turkey, Ben. Plenty there,' Dominic says, piling more meat on Ben's plate.

As if intuiting that her owner needs rescuing, Lou scratches at the rug. Susannah excuses herself from the table to attend to the dogs. She closes the dining room door behind her and opens the front door just wide enough for the dogs to get back in while she slips into Dominic's study.

The manuscript sits in a neat pile beside his typewriter. She glances through the first page, and then skims quickly through the following pages. He has reinvented himself. His parents are exaggerated versions of themselves; caricatures. Dominic has a skill for description that is by turns florid, contemptuous and excessive. He prides himself on his ability to employ an unlikely adjective or metaphor. His descriptions of Michelle are ludicrous – pure fantasy. He's transformed a plump little hausfrau from South London into Aphrodite herself. Michelle is a social worker now; she'll be mortified by these intimate revelations. Happy Valley, what on earth? Oh no, that's just disgusting.

Susannah flicks quickly through to her own meeting with Dominic. Reading it, she feels a flush of hot shame. His description of their first tryst, which admittedly did take place in an under-stairs cupboard at a party, is described in the most lurid terms. They had done none of the things he details – practices she was probably unaware of at the time. It was a drunken fumble of clothing pulled aside followed by a damp coupling in the most traditional sense. Sordid. Thank God Maxwell isn't alive to read this description of him amusing guests mere yards away from his treacherous wife. He will be posthumously humiliated.

Dominic's gleeful tone makes her wonder if it was jealousy of Maxwell's success that fuelled the relentless pursuit and seduction of his wife. Dominic was always careless with other people in a way that Maxwell never was. Yet here, woven into the subtext, Dominic has managed to make himself sound almost admirable as a man of passion and action. She feels fury and disgust both at him and herself for her collusion in this conceit.

Why had she betrayed Maxwell so brutally? It occurs to her now, for the first time, that she too was jealous. Jealous of the time Max invested in other people. She was punishing him for being so loved by all around him. She doesn't even want to find out how Dominic worms his way out of the Farash affair. She picks up the entire manuscript, fans out the pages and pushes it into the dying embers of the fire. She prods it with the poker until the flame catches and, one by one, the pages curl into blackened transparency and collapse as ash.

Chapter Thirty-five

Dominic is rather enjoying his place at the head of the table, envisaging himself as a man of substance. Given she has become so slovenly around the house, Susannah has pulled out all stops. The dining table is festooned as though for a themed dinner on a cruise ship with jolly red-and-green napkins, bunches of holly and mistletoe. The Royal Doulton has been dusted off, the candelabras gleam, dignified despite the garish red candles stuck in them at odd angles. It's all a little tasteless and excessive but guest-appropriate (the antipodeans have probably never experienced a traditional Christmas) and, all in all, creates a pleasing ambience.

Without offspring, he and Susannah have never experienced a family Christmas of their own making. One of the bonuses of leaving England was not having to spend Christmas with Rebecca and her supercilious husband, or listen to Reggie's interminable stories about the washing-machine business and his dead relatives. Now here is Dominic, with his clan gathered around him.

Mia, with her pent-up expression, adds nothing to the *joie de vivre*. Susannah has been simmering with resentment all day, and even Ben is in the grip of a gloomy mood. Roxy is the only one who sparkles at this gathering. Her father's daughter, able to rise to any occasion.

He knows he overstepped the mark openly criticising Susannah like that, and when she returns from letting the dogs out, he will set things right with a fulsome apology. Despite the odd *contretemps* with Her Ladyship recently, he's been very content tucked away in his study working on his book. It has been transformative to re-examine his whole life and discover that he has achieved far more than he realised. It's been a quiet time of reflection and he will miss living each day in the comforting embrace of his own story.

Right now he is actually feeling a little under the weather, probably as a result of drinking too early in the day, having got a head start prior to the arrival of their guests. The art of pacing is something he prides himself on. Timed right, he has the ability to drink steadily for hours without ill effect. Perhaps another indignity of old age is a loss of capacity.

Now that Susannah has disappeared, the conversation seems to comprise snippets of unrelated topics, as if no one has the energy to pursue vigorous discourse. God knows where the woman has gone. She must have taken the mutts out for a ramble, leaving him to shoulder the social burden and her guests all sitting at the table none the wiser. She's become positively feral in the last year, appearing to have lost touch with what is socially acceptable.

'Ben was telling me you have a valuable Jacobean chair,' says Roxy, apropos of nothing as far as Dominic can make out.

He notices Mia shoot Ben a look of disbelief for some reason. Odd girl.

'Yes, it's a family heirloom . . .' Dominic gets up, slides opens the double doors and looks around the living room. 'Where is it? Bloody Susannah, always changing the room around.' The chair is definitely not in the room. In fact, he can't remember when he last saw the thing. Someone tried to sit in it recently, when was that? His head swims as he tries to remember the details of the incident. 'Where's my chair?' he asks when Susannah reappears.

'I put it upstairs, out of the way,' she says, sitting back down at the table.

'I'd love to see it before I go,' says Roxy. 'I'm leaving early doors tomorrow.'

'You obviously have some private timetable you're working to,' says Dominic. 'Here today, gone tomorrow.'

Roxy laughs. 'Work to do. Do you think you'll come back to the UK at some point?'

'We may be forced to if the British government stops paying pensions overseas,' says Dominic.

'Dominic can't go back, but I think you already know that,' says Susannah. Dominic gives her a warning frown, gesturing dismissively in her direction in an attempt to brush the comment away. Typical of her to start trouble five minutes after negotiating a truce.

'Yes, I am aware of the story; we've talked it through,' says Roxy.

'Dominic's version —' says Susannah.

'And I saw the story in the papers too, of course,' adds Roxy.

'Do we need this conflict now?' asks Dominic. 'It's Christmas.

Goodwill to all men, including this one. That's the last topic we need to discuss.'

'You won't get the truth out of him,' says Susannah.

'You don't need to bore everyone with the details, Susannah. Perhaps you're overtired and in need of a nice lie down?'

'The papers don't know the half of it,' continues Susannah, undeterred. 'It was a war over a parking space. The lovely and blameless Mr Farash died because of a parking space.'

'Shut up, Susannah. You've obviously had too much to drink and now you're making a fool of yourself.'

'Woah, Dominic,' says Ben. 'I know you're a bit drunk, man, maybe you both are, but —'

'It's not as though I murdered the man, for Christ's sake! I didn't know a thing about it until people started laying wreaths outside the place.'

'What do you mean about the parking space?' Roxy asks Susannah. 'That wasn't in the papers. There was something about the Farash family disputing whether Dominic ate there —'

'Oh, for God's sake, take no notice. Susannah is a rich repository of conspiracy theories. "Nothing is quite what it seems".' Dominic mimes the quotation marks with his fingers, a gesture he despises. 'Let's move on to lighter subjects.'

'I think we'd better go,' says Mia, turning to Ben, who immediately pushes back his chair.

'No, no,' Dominic insists. 'I apologise for our silly squabble. My fault entirely. We haven't even had dessert yet, our pavlovian masterpiece created by Mia, Queen of the Dessert.'

Roxy at least laughs at his little joke but the Tinkers are still poised to flee. Susannah's scowl is the full Churchill, only needing a fat cigar and a homburg to complete the bulldog look.

Insisting everyone relax, Dominic gets up and gathers the plates neatly, the way he's seen a thousand waiters stack them over the years, and takes it all to the kitchen in a teetering pile. But it's not dessert that's on his mind.

Dumping the plates in the sink, he goes straight up the stairs and checks the spare room. Nothing. Susannah's door is locked. He feels around the top of the door frame. Looks under the vase on the hall table, tips the vase upside down and the key falls into his hand.

In contrast to downstairs, where she has recovered the situation, her room is chaotic with the bed unmade, clothes and all her belongings strewn about. No sign of the chair but it appears his wife will shortly be going on a long journey across the sea. And not for a holiday, either. There are two large suitcases and several boxes half packed.

There's a stack of papers on her desk. He rifles through them, discarding as he goes, no need to be covert since he'll be confronting her the moment their guests depart. They'll have this out for once and for all. In his hand is a bank statement, the account in Susannah's maiden name with almost six thousand euros in it. There's a dozen deposits and two withdrawals. His first thought is that Reggie has come through with some funds after all. He sits down on the bed trying to focus but he's had far too much to drink and the figures skitter across the page. No, that can't be right. If it came from Reggie, the deposits wouldn't be in these varying amounts with odd cents.

He notices a manila folder propped up at the back of the desk and picks it up. There's half-a-dozen printouts of statements from selectwinesales.com. She's secretly buying wine! He's impressed by her good taste, some of his expertise must have rubbed off.

There's a Domaine Romanée-Conti! He owns two bottles of Romanée-Conti, a gift from Serge's when it first opened to pave the way for the glowing review that put them on the map. Some might call it a bribe but it was well deserved and he has no regrets in that regard.

Then all at once the sober reality hits him. She's not buying, she's *selling*. She's selling *his* Romanée-Conti. And here's *his* Vieux Château Certan and *his* Dujac Clos de la Roche!

He takes a deep breath and tries to marshal his thoughts and calm himself. It's as though he's just dropped acid and is having a very, very bad trip. It's not visions of sugar plums that dance in his head but wine bottles walking their way out of his cellar. His mind expands and contracts, information rises to the surface but before he can grasp it, it's gone. He's losing his own grip on reality.

Finally, one clear thought makes itself known. She is not doing this alone. She has the help of someone and that someone is one of the Tinkers – or both. He is surrounded by traitors; in a nest of scorpions. He's startled by the trill of the phone beside the bed. Oh, so the telephone is apparently back on as well!

'Dominic? It's Michelle,' says a voice he hasn't heard for thirty years.

'Michelle? This is unexpected,' he says, stating the obvious, and realising in the same moment that he's struggling with the pace of change.

'Dominic, it's about Roxanne . . .'

'Roxy, yes, she's here now, do you want to speak to her?'

'Look, I'm sorry. I've only just found out about this. It never would have happened if I'd known. I would have put a stop to it. She's only just admitted it to me and I called straight away.'

'Oh, don't worry about it,' says Dominic. 'It was a shock but it's all worked out for the best. Good to get to know my daughter. Should have done it years ago.'

There's a long silence on the end of the line. Finally, Michelle says, 'Dominic, I'm awfully sorry but your daughter's right here. That woman is not Roxanne. She's an imposter. Look, I know it's dreadful and you'll think badly of Rox but she was offered silly money by the paper. She's . . . she's got a lot of money troubles. I know that's no excuse. We haven't really been on speaking terms . . . well, I won't go into that but she's here with me today and . . . she's had an attack of the guilts. I don't suppose you'll ever want to meet her now.'

Dominic sits down heavily on the bed, straining to make sense of what Michelle is saying. He's reached saturation point. Does this have anything to do with the theft of his wine? There seems to be no confluence between the two, not that he can immediately see at least. Unless Roxy is the one conspiring to steal his wine? Why would someone want to impersonate his daughter? Who would do such a thing? Michelle must be mistaken. 'Wait a minute, are you quite certain this is *not* Roxy?'

'Absolutely. Her name is Joanna Smyth. Roxanne's known her forever – they went through school together, that's how she knows so much about you. She's a journalist now with one of the trashy tabloids. She put the story forward and Roxy got on board. There's been renewed interest with the lawsuit and everything.'

'Lawsuit?' It's as though he's watching five televisions on different channels. He's sweating so profusely he picks up a towel off the floor to mop his face.

'The Farash children are apparently taking out a defamation lawsuit against you and the paper. You must know about it. You can probably look it up online. You should get in touch with your solicitor, find out what's happening. Look, I'm so sorry. Roxanne sends her apologies. She does realise she was wrong. I'm amazed Joanna managed to carry it off. It was her idea to come to you at Christmas; she thought it would be more convincing.'

Outraged, Dominic finds his voice: '"More convincing"? I didn't need convincing! I'm not in the habit of asking visitors for proof of identity – I was convinced from the start! Why wouldn't I be convinced? What's not to be convinced about?!'

'All right, don't shout at me. I rang you the minute I found out. I've rung a dozen times and I've rung her but she won't pick up. Wait a minute . . . oh dear . . .' She covers the microphone so he can hear only muffled conversation. 'Dominic, look, apparently they're planning to send a photographer out there, probably early in the new year. So watch out for that. They're very intrusive. They'll go through your bins. Keep the doors locked and the curtains drawn. I really am terribly sorry. Good luck! And, well, Merry Christmas.'

Dominic hangs up the phone and lies down on the bed trying to get his bearings. After a few minutes he gets up and staggers into the ensuite and splashes his face with cold water. A boiling disorienting rage pumps through him, forcing sweat out of every pore. There are so many things to be angry about he doesn't know where to start. Right now he's worried about having a stroke. His blood pressure must be through the roof. He sits down. Takes long deep breaths. Calms himself from a boiling fury, down, down, down, to steely resolve.

As he goes back downstairs, the first part of his plan quickly comes together. He walks into the living room just in time to see Joanna pick up her phone and give it a puzzled look. He has to strike now. The other three are still in the dining room; they'll keep for the moment.

'Put that down, my dear. Come and help me choose a Sauternes to accompany dessert.' He wraps a fatherly arm around her shoulders. She looks taken back; he's never once touched her. But now he is and that's the risk you take when you impersonate someone's daughter. 'What a shame you're leaving tomorrow,' he purrs. 'It's been a dream come true having you here.'

She reluctantly puts her phone down but prevaricates; her vermin instinct senses something is off. 'Do we really need more wine? Won't I need a coat?'

Dominic grabs a throw rug from the sofa and wraps it tenderly around her shoulders as he walks her towards the conservatory door. 'We'll only be a minute,' he assures her.

As they walk down the back path, she continues to protest lamely. 'I honestly think I've had enough wine for one day. I have a long drive in the morning.'

Dominic keeps his arm firmly around her shoulders as he reaches for the key hidden in the brickwork near the door. He opens the door and switches on the light. 'The Sauternes are along here to the left,' he says, guiding her deeper into the cellar. Now she's here, he can't even be bothered discussing her treachery, her criminal ambition. He simply leads her to the rack, places a bottle in her hands and while she's distracted, flicks off the light and leaves, taking the spare key from the hook with him and letting the door slam shut behind him. That's her out of the way for the moment. Now for his treacherous wife.

Chapter Thirty-six

The atmosphere in the Harringtons' house is toxic and, on top of being up most of the night, it's making me feel sick. Ben is still so distant with me. Roxy is acting cheerful. Susannah's all over the place. And Dominic – there is something really frightening about him. He has this underlying aggression, like a dangerous animal waiting for its moment to pounce. It feels like we are all on the brink of a disaster that can't be avoided. Dominic and Susannah have both been drinking heavily and it doesn't take any imagination to work out how things might go as the day wears on. To be here with these awful strangers at Christmas, it's like we have put ourselves into purgatory.

Dominic and Roxy have now both disappeared and Susannah, for some strange reason, is explaining to Ben in painful detail how to make an authentic cassoulet. He looks like he's going to lose consciousness at any moment. While that's going on, I leave the table and go to the kitchen to assemble the pavlova. As I cross the living room, I notice Dominic standing on the patio with a small chainsaw in his hand. What could he possibly be doing with this right in the middle of lunch – cutting more wood for the fire? He starts up the chainsaw. For a moment it looks as though he's doing a bit of pruning, but why now? Then I realise what's happening and shout for Susannah.

Susannah and Ben rush in from the dining room just in time to see Dominic systematically demolishing the pergola. He hacks through each of the thick stems of the climbing roses then attacks the latticework. It's getting dark outside but we can still see his furious expression. The only sound is the shriek of the chainsaw straining in its work.

We stand watching in silent shock. As soon as Ben makes a move for the door, Susannah comes to life and grabs his arm, screaming, 'Don't go out there! Oh my God! Where are the dogs? Where are the dogs?! Lock the door!'

I find the dogs cowering under the sofa. 'It's all right, they're here.' I wonder where Roxy is, not that I really care, but her handbag is on the floor and her phone on the table, so I assume she's in the bathroom.

'I don't know what to do,' says Ben, rubbing his head the way he does when he's agitated. 'He's gone completely mad. What's wrong with him?'

Susannah cries out as the chainsaw rips through her beloved arbour seat, reducing it to kindling. Dominic moves on with a sense of urgency, leaving a trail of destruction; smashed pieces of lattice and rose canes cover the ground. As he cuts through one of the posts holding up the pergola, a piece of the archway swings down and catches him across the forehead, leaving a bright red slash of blood. Ben sees his moment and, in a flash, he's out the door and across the patio. Before Dominic realises what's happening, Ben hooks his forearm around Dominic's neck, jerking his head backwards, forcing him to drop the chainsaw.

Ben pulls Dominic to the ground, holding him there while he turns off the chainsaw. For a moment, all is silent, then Susannah starts making the most horrific wailing sound. I wish I could say something comforting but there's nothing to be said, it's not going to be all right. Dominic has gone completely insane.

Ben takes Dominic's arm, gets him on his feet and helps him inside. The cut on his forehead drips blood down his face, his shoulders slump, and he looks less like a dangerous maniac than a pensioner who's taken a tumble. Both Susannah and I stand back as he passes, as if we think he'll lash out at us. Ben leads him to the sofa, gets his jacket off, and sits him down.

'Can you get a towel and some water?' Ben asks Susannah while he examines the wound. 'Then we can see how deep it is. Do you have any painkillers?'

'Does he need an ambulance?' I ask, hoping they might cart him away.

'No, I don't bloody need an ambulance!' snaps Dominic. 'What I need is the *gendarmes* to lay charges against you three!'

Susannah arrives with the towel, water and a blister pack of tablets. But Dominic bats away Ben's attempts to mop up the blood on his face. 'Get away from me, you bastard!'

'What the hell are you talking about?' asks Ben, more confused than angry. 'Maybe we do need an ambulance.'

'This is what happens when you mix with the criminal classes,' says Dominic furiously. 'Next thing you know they're pilfering the silver or, in this case, thousands of pounds' worth of my wine. Scum, filthy thieving scum!' He turns on Susannah. 'And you, you evil bitch – where's my fucking chair?'

Susannah covers her face with her hands and collapses into an armchair sobbing loudly.

'Hold it. Are you accusing us?' asks Ben. 'What are you talking about? You've got your wires crossed, Dominic.' He gestures helplessly towards the destruction outside. 'Is this what all that was about? I don't even know what you're talking about.'

Dominic turns his gaze on me with a grim smile. 'It was you, wasn't it? Not him. He knew nothing about it. I suspected as much. You thieving little bitch.'

Ben takes a handful of Dominic's shirt-front, twists it and half lifts him off the sofa. 'Hey! Listen, mate, I know you're pretty pissed but that's enough, one more word —'

'She was helping me!' interrupts Susannah. 'Where do you think the money for the food came from? The electricity? Petrol?' She stops abruptly and looks around. 'Where's Roxy? Dominic! Where is she? She's got nothing to do with it.'

'She's in London, as it happens,' says Dominic, snatching the towel from Ben and dabbing at his wound. 'That woman is an imposter. A journalist from the gutter press.'

'What?! You have absolutely lost it,' says Ben. 'You've definitely got that wrong. That's not possible.' He turns to me with a helpless look, as if I can shed some light on this confusing situation but I'm staying right out of it.

'Who told you that, Dominic?' asks Susannah.

'Michelle. She rang earlier. It's no good arguing with me. It's a fact.'

'What's her real name then?' asks Ben, reaching into his pocket.

'Joanna Smyth.'

Ben taps the name into his phone. He stares at it for a moment and slowly puts it back in his pocket. 'He's right. She's a journo. Writes for *Exposé* magazine.'

'What have you done with her?' Susannah shouts. 'Dominic! Where is she?'

'Oh, stop your caterwauling, you stupid woman. I haven't chopped her up, much as I'd like to. She's in the cellar, which is a desecration in itself. Key's in my jacket. Send her packing before I'm tempted to do something violent.'

Susannah fumbles in Dominic's jacket pocket and goes stumbling out the back door. Dominic pops out painkillers, one after the other, and stuffs them in his mouth and throws down the glass of water. He stretches out on the sofa with a groan and mutters angrily under his breath about the treachery he's suffered. 'Let's just get one thing clear,' he says to no one in particular. 'I am the victim here.'

I grab Ben's arm. 'Let's go home.' He nods, still looking bewildered. Just then, not-Roxy comes storming into the room. She is almost unrecognisable. It's not just that she's been unmasked and all pretence of niceness has fallen away; her face is red and swollen from crying and her hands are filthy as though she's been trying to dig her way out. She looks around wildly, sees Dominic lying on the sofa, and shouts: 'I have claustrophobia, you fucking lunatic! I could have you charged for that. Abduction!'

Oddly, she seems more like his daughter now than she ever did when she was pretending to be. There's a delayed reaction from Dominic and I wonder if it was a good idea for him to take so many painkillers on top of all the alcohol he's had.

'Go ahead,' he slurs, all the fight gone out of him. 'Do your worst, it's all copy, isn't it? Substandard . . . third-rate,

I'll warrant. Is there a reason you're still here? Don't you have what you need? Get out.'

'I will do my worst, and you can judge for yourself when the story comes out.' She grabs her bag, rifles through it and looks around the room.

I'm the closest one to her phone. I pick it up and hand it to Ben. He can decide what he wants to do. He snaps the back open and removes the sim card. 'There you go,' he says, tossing the phone to her. 'You heard what he said, get out.'

She's pretty tough but for a moment she looks wounded. Then she turns away and walks down the hall without looking back.

Through the windows we can see Susannah standing among the ruins of her pergola clutching Lou and Chou in her arms. Much as I want to go out and comfort the poor woman, I need to go home much more. I want to feel Ben's comforting arms around me and never set foot in this house again.

Chapter Thirty-seven

Susannah is so broken she barely has the strength to climb the stairs to her room but the fear of Dominic waking now that she's alone in the house with him is incentive enough. Her bedroom door is wide open and papers from her desk are scattered on the floor. She locks the door behind her and sinks to her knees, her body racked with uncontrollable sobbing. When it passes, she curls up on her side, drained of emotion. She wishes that something would happen, that some greater power would take her life from her and it would end here. Lou and Chou fret and whimper, licking her hands and face. She can't abandon them. She has to find the strength to move. And she has to find it now.

She gets to her feet and looks out the window: it's pouring with rain and darkness is falling. Driving back to England tonight is beyond her capability, but the time for excuses is over. She doesn't need to drive all the way. Toulouse is an hour away, she can stay the night there and leave first thing in the morning. She'd rather sleep in the car tonight than stay here. She'll be home by nightfall tomorrow. The prospect of entering her father's safe, predictable world has become so overwhelmingly glorious, that's what she needs to hold on to.

She quickly gathers her things together. Two suitcases only, she'll abandon the rest for the moment. Dominic being conked out on the sofa actually suits her purpose. She can slip downstairs and out through the kitchen door without detection. With a frenetic energy, somewhere between purpose and panic, she rams the rest of her clothes into the suitcases and forces them shut. Not wanting the dogs to whimper and wake him, she carries them downstairs first. In the kitchen she packs snacks and a bowl for water for them. She settles the pugs in the back seat of the car and tucks a warm blanket around them. 'We're going on an adventure, my darlings,' she whispers, fervently wishing she believed it.

Back upstairs, she takes a final look around her room and wonders if she has spent a single happy moment there. Not that she can remember, but this is no time for reflection, it's a time for action. She throws the bank statements and personal papers into a bag and slowly, carefully and quietly, carries the suitcases downstairs. She takes a quick peek into the darkness of the living room, lit only by the dying embers of the fire. No movement. No sound.

The car is packed, all is ready. She runs through a mental checklist and stops to wonder what she did with the keys to the cellar. She had been so frantic and upset when she let the pretend Roxy out, the order of events is confused. She remembers having both keys in her hand. Remembers propping the door open. Did she leave them on the alcove table for Dominic as she meant to? He will really go berserk if she leaves with the keys. She takes the torch from the boot of the car and walks quietly down the side path to the cellar. A quick flash of the torch into the alcove confirms both keys are on the table, and she hurries back to the car.

Consumed by fear, she takes off at a clip and drives into the night sobbing so hard she frightens herself, as well as the dogs who stand on the back seat barking shrilly. She has to stop herself somehow, or pull over before something terrible happens. Slowing down, she flicks open the glovebox, feels around inside, finds a CD and pushes it into the player. Breathless half-formed words tumble from her lips. By the second chorus, somewhere between laughter and tears, she's yelling the lyrics she knows off by heart, drowning out Fleetwood Mac at the top of her voice, and for three and a half minutes she feels a little better.

Chapter Thirty-eight

Peering through the tiny ventilation grille of the cellar, Dominic sees the brake lights of the Audi suspended in the blackness. Gravel explodes beneath the tyres as the car accelerates at speed, out of the yard and onto the road. The night is silent apart from the sound of his car receding into the distance.

Less than half an hour ago, he'd awoken from his stupor to find himself lying on the sofa, still a little drunk and dazed, and the house in darkness. He'd lain there for a while, clarifying the situation in his own mind and considering his next move. Clearly the guests had gone and Susannah had skulked off to her room. To say Christmas Day had been a disaster was an understatement. Even with a little distance, the whole experience was like one of those ghastly American comedies, only missing someone being electrocuted by decorative lights, which, all things considered, might have livened things up. He would have thoroughly enjoyed seeing Joanna–Roxy take 240 volts for her efforts.

It was incredible how well she had ingratiated herself. How he so trustingly confided in her – read her excerpts from his memoir.

Thank God his book was finished and his version of his story now intact. It dawned on him then, that much as having the Farash business dragged up again by the press was disagreeable, it would have publishers gagging for his memoir. He'd felt almost gleeful that fate had played into his hands. But the first priority was to make sure that that faithless cow of a wife didn't help herself to any more of his cellar. To that end, he had abandoned the comfort of the sofa and, despite his throbbing head, slipped on his jacket. He could hear Susannah moving about upstairs and he quickly made his way out the conservatory door and down the back path.

The alcove was dark and he thought it prudent to leave the outside light off. Susannah had carelessly left the door to the cellar propped open. He turned the cellar light on, quickly located a couple of cartons and began to pack some of his best vintages. It soon became obvious that Susannah had been rearranging bottles to hide her thieving. Who knew that she possessed the wit for such deviousness? He'd have to do a complete audit, find out exactly what was missing. In fact, once he sorted out the hiccup with the Tinkers, he'd get Ben to check the value of some of the better vintages.

The safest place to store the wines was his study with its locking door. He carried the first carton out of the cellar but as he stepped out of the shelter of the alcove, he saw the bouncing light of a torch coming down the side path. In a moment of panic, he rushed back into the cellar, flicked off the light and pulled the door closed. He waited to see if Susannah had her own key and would open the door, in which case she'd get a nasty shock. But he would be ready for her.

He absentmindedly patted his pocket to reassure himself that the key was there. It wasn't. Putting the carton down, he plunged his hands into both pockets simultaneously, then his breast pocket and trouser pockets. There was a slow realisation, and something half-remembered about the spare key. He turned on the light and stood staring for the longest time at the empty hook.

The silence of the cellar, previously music to his ears, became immediately oppressive. There was no point in panicking. That's what had got him into this fix. Sooner or later Susannah would realise that he was missing and liberate him. Unless she decided to leave him here. She wouldn't have the intestinal fortitude to see that through.

The temperature in the cellar was cold but stable. He wouldn't freeze to death but it was hardly an ideal place to spend the night. Exhausted by his labours of the day, particularly the pruning exercise, he decided to flatten out some cartons to make something of a bed and cover himself up the way homeless people did.

He had heard the sound of the Audi engine starting and went to the ventilation grille, which was just above ground level in the courtyard. He saw the reversing lights reflected off the wall and was seized by a feeling he had never experienced before. As though he was standing outside himself watching his own response. This must be what people described as a panic attack. He actually felt like screaming. Not just felt like it, enacted it. He shouted himself hoarse even knowing it was a waste of time. The only possible reason Susannah could be setting off at that time of the night was because she was leaving him. Her bags were already packed. She simply needed to zip them up and go.

Now he finds himself standing on a crate gazing blindly out the ventilation grille into the thick gloom of the night. Now she has gone, nobody will look for him. No one will wonder about him. The Tinkers won't come back. He has disgraced himself. An adjective that could equally apply to his whole life. He has imprisoned himself. Life imprisonment, in fact, because it's highly unlikely that anyone at all will come to the house in the next few days, or even weeks.

So here he is, hoist with his own petard. Caught in his own trap. The only question that remains is whether he will die of starvation or hypothermia. He contemplates which will be slower and more dreadful as he paces the length and breadth of the cellar. Walking up and down each of the three tunnels, he checks the walls, the floor and the ceilings, imagining a secret escape hatch revealing itself for the first time. He tries pulling at the door, but knows this is futile. He wanted the cellar secure and he got it.

Old people are always bellyaching about wanting to die in their own home, but clearly not in their cellar. In the comfort of their bed, surrounded by loved ones. That will not be his fate. He will breathe his last breath on a bed of cardboard like a common tramp.

He gets back on the crate and pushes his nose against the cold grille and looks up into the night sky. Rain falls steadily, no star or moon to be seen. He feels the icy air on his cheeks. He smells the mud outside and wonders at the complexity of that not unpleasant odour, made more beautiful simply because it is a part of the world outside from which he is forever excluded.

Susannah is most likely on her way to England, running off home to Daddy. Sooner or later she will try to contact him and, no doubt, want to put the house on the market. Some months from now, someone will come to clear the place out and find his body. He feels a little cheered by the idea that this person could be Susannah, only disappointed that he won't be alive to witness her reaction.

It makes him furious that she will get her hands on his wine after all. It is entirely her fault that he's trapped in here. If she hadn't been stealing from him he wouldn't have come down here to hide his wines. If she hadn't come down to steal more wine, he wouldn't have rushed into the cellar and locked himself in. Why did he do that instead of confronting her? What was she going to do, wrestle them off him? It was a reflex action, a natural response in the circumstance.

He almost can't be bothered to be angry at Susannah; he's worn himself out on that one. He has bigger problems. Or does he? Or is it that he has no problems? Is it that his time has come and all the problems of the corporeal world – lawsuits, divorces, bankruptcy, slanderous stories – are now irrelevant. Now that he faces his own mortality, he wishes he were more spiritual and could experience it on a higher plane.

He realises all at once that there is a third way to die. Infinitely more pleasant than starvation or hypothermia, and borderline spiritual. Alcohol poisoning. He will poison himself with some of the best wines in the world. It's almost Shakespearean in its tragic irony. He will work his way through his best vintages; wines he probably never would have consumed because they are simply too valuable to drink. He has everything he needs at hand including a corkscrew and a tasting glass. What a way to go out! He feels positively elated. His death will be a spiritual experience like no other. A time of quiet focus, contemplation and reflection.

He folds and rips up empty cartons, like a rat making a nest, and packs them into one corner until he has somewhere agreeable to sit and enjoy the experience. He's excited to discover the rug that he had so considerately wrapped around that wretched woman's shoulders, discarded on the floor, and adds that to his nest.

He spends quite some time debating aloud the selection of his final drops. He sets them out in order. Although some of the vintages don't really need it, he pulls the cork on each of the reds to allow them to breathe. By the third bottle he'll probably be too drunk to get up, let alone make another selection and open it. Better to have the whole thing planned out nicely in advance. He yearns for a little *foie gras* or a sliver of cheese to enhance the experience but it is not to be and he accepts that with an equanimity that he can't help but admire. What a shame his final hours won't be documented in his memoir; that would be a nice twist. Perhaps someone could ghostwrite that part for him? Or at least add an epilogue detailing the tragic circumstances of his death.

He has a couple of bottles of Cristal put aside and, at the current temperature of the cellar, the champagne would be perfect for drinking. But then again, he doesn't want to fill up on bubbles and peak too early, thereby not being able to completely appreciate the first red, which will be the pinnacle of his collection, the remaining la Romanée-Conti. So he decides to skip the Cristal and go straight to the *vin rouge*.

Given that he wouldn't have drunk both of the Romanée, he feels less distressed by the thought of Susannah flogging one. He settles down in his little nook, wipes out the glass carefully with the corner of his shirt, pours the wine, inhales deeply and takes his first sip, carefully savouring every nuance. It is, just as he anticipated, almost a religious experience. It's as though every wine he sampled in his life has brought him to this moment, educated his palate to appreciate the multi-dimensioned character of this nectar.

As he drinks, he ponders his life and the story he has documented and feels a deep sense of satisfaction that he has put the work in and left a legacy. Even the manner of his death will be very attractive to a publisher. And if someone was to do their homework and tot up the cost of his exit plan, they would discover it was well over the ten-thousand-pound mark, perhaps more. He will be published posthumously. Readers will mourn his passing. He was a real character, they will say. Like a good wine. Ironically, Joanna's story will help sell his book, so she'll actually be working for him instead of against him. It was a shame the way it all turned out. He had rather liked her.

The first bottle goes down smoothly over the next hour as he takes his time with it. Sitting with his back against the wall, he looks around with a renewed appreciation for the construction of the cellar. He admires the workmanship of the bricks that form the arches and even goes so far as to examine them closely, wondering if they had been fired in a local kiln. Now he'll never know and there's something restful in that sense of finality. His thoughts wander in a pleasant, almost mystical, way that is quite new to him.

Towards the end of the second bottle, he begins to feel a little maudlin. He finds himself more concerned about the hereafter, wondering if there is one. He'd been brought up a Catholic and, regardless of how lapsed one was, there was always the niggling worry they might be right.

His conscience begins to bother him. All this time he's been telling himself that Farash had a choice. No need to fall on his sword. He could have just parked his car somewhere else, for

Christ's sake! How difficult could it possibly be? Then the whole episode could have been avoided and the man would still be alive, poppaduming to his heart's content. Now facing his own imminent demise, Dominic can admit to himself that he isn't proud of the part he played; his mean-spiritedness, his spite, his dishonesty. He thinks back to the beginning and wonders how things might have played out differently.

The King of Kashmir had been right opposite the Harringtons' house and, from the bay window of the living room, they had a clear view into the interior of the restaurant. Although nothing flash, it was a celebrity haunt and Dominic would see Farash come out of the restaurant to meet chauffeur-driven limos, ushering the occupants inside, bowing and scraping like a servant. It had annoyed him when Farash bought a Rolls Royce. He didn't care about him being Indian, it was simply that the man just didn't know his place. He seemed to think that a great lumbering Rolls Royce would make him a toff or a celebrity like his customers. Typical of people who hob-nob with celebs and soon begin to believe they are one. Farash behaved as though he actually *was* the king of Kashmir.

Directly outside the restaurant was a bus stop and therefore no parking. Prior to his extravagant purchase, Farash, who lived with his family in a flat above the restaurant, had been satisfied to park his clapped-out old Jag off down the street. But he was so proud of his Roller, he insisted on parking it opposite the restaurant – directly outside the Harrington residence – where he could admire it and keep it in full view of his clientele. Every few days, the son, a boy in his twenties, would bring a bucket and wash the gritty black crust of London air off it, drying it lovingly with a chamois until it glowed.

Living above the restaurant, Farash often went for days without using the car and Dominic's frustration began to build day by day. The minute he saw Farash get behind the wheel, smugly infatuated with his own stateliness, Dominic would be out the door at an unseemly pace to collect his own car parked up the street. He'd be in a lather to get back to the contentious spot before some other driver nabbed it. All that aside, the sweet relief when he secured that spot, knowing that Farash would be cursing in Punjabi or whatever it was he spoke, made all the effort worthwhile.

It wasn't as though Dominic hadn't tried to reason with him. He went with the high-handed approach first: 'Look, Farash, you can't park your car there. It's right outside my house. I've had to park two streets away.'

'I have a parking permit,' Farash assured him. 'I can park wherever I choose. That is the law. You should be very proud to have this beautiful beast outside your house. What a splendid view you have! And at no cost to you.'

'Yes, well, beauty is in the eye of the beholder. The fact is that it's a matter of common courtesy not to park right outside someone else's property.'

'I am not aware of this courtesy. This is a street owned by the public. I am a member of the public. So are you. Sometimes you park here. Sometimes I park here. This is very fair, I think.' His tone was careful and polite, punctuated by alternating smiles and frowns.

This was the first of many such conversations. All of which irked Dominic. Farash seemed to think that Dominic should be honoured to live in such close proximity to the King of Kashmir, as if he enjoyed views of the Taj itself instead of a bog-standard shopfront with its name painted in gold 'Indian' calligraphy across the window. Farash had invited Dominic to come and dine at the restaurant as his guest and see for himself that this was the best Kashmiri cuisine in London. Of course, the man was unaware that he was talking to one of the nation's most highly esteemed food critics.

Regardless of how rude and aggressive Dominic was towards Farash, the man continued to be both courteous and uncompromising. Dominic tried digging in, leaving his car there and using buses, taxis and the tube. But this was highly inconvenient, not to mention expensive.

Susannah had not one iota of interest in or sympathy for Dominic's skirmishes with Farash. Despite up-to-the-minute commentary on the escalating situation, she continued to believe that Farash and his family were lovely people. Typical of her indiscriminate approval – no insight whatsoever into the dark souls of her fellow human beings.

Over the years, Dominic had written some scathing reviews, and he had closed down at least half-a-dozen restaurants that were, in any case, a blight. He performed a public service by clearing out the dross. The King of Kashmir was not one of those and the truth was that he had never eaten there. He went over one morning before it opened, peered inside and read the blackboard menu. He then put his imagination to work, documenting his non-existent experience with vivid description, metaphor and a sprinkling of apt adjectives. He typed it up and called it through to the paper. It was one of his more incisive pieces, partly because he had free rein, unconstrained by truth or accuracy. He wishes he could remember it now, but only fragments remain: something about the burrah kebab grilled lamb chops having the flavour of something rescued from a house fire, a sizzling synthetic taste. The salmon tikka, so dry that a hacksaw would have been more useful than a knife. The soft-shell crab coated in wallpaper glue and dusted with scorched remnants from the aforementioned house fire.

Just to make sure, he made an appointment with his doctor and fabricated a lurid account of illness. He based his symptoms on a previous bout of food poisoning that had actually been contracted in India, so was loosely related to Farash. Naturally in the interests of public service, this had to be reported to the appropriate authorities. By that stage, he had become so caught up in his story, he had almost forgotten it was a fiction. He even felt a little bilious, which just goes to show the power of the mind.

While he'd had the satisfaction of being instrumental in the closure of those other restaurants, he'd never actually had the pleasure of watching it happen. Quite quickly, there were indications that all was not well. This, presumably, was because his reviews now appeared *on*line, communicating faster with more people.

Where it had been famously difficult to obtain a table, within weeks, empty tables proliferated. The limos gradually disappeared. A month later the King of Kashmir began to close one, then two nights a week, when it had previously been open every night. Farash himself could be seen some afternoons, standing in the doorway smoking pensively, looking up and down the street as if trying to make sense of this downturn. Dominic wondered if he had actually seen the review and considered slipping a clipping under the door. If by some remote chance Farash hadn't seen it, the mysterious drop in his popularity would be a humbling experience for him; perhaps he would interpret it as a karmic reprisal for his former pomposity. Dominic would not be the one to enlighten him.

The final victory was slow to dawn. On a couple of occasions, Dominic had noticed a fellow looking the Roller over. He was accompanied not by Farash himself but the son, and Dominic was quietly confident that this chap was a potential buyer.

When Dominic came downstairs one morning and saw the parking space empty, he left it that way. Over the next couple of days, various cars parked there for short periods, their owners unaware that this tiny patch of London was disputed territory. By the end of the week it was clear that the Roller was gone and victory was his for the taking.

It was an empty victory to some degree because no one cared about it the way he did. There was no one with whom to celebrate. Susannah had not shown an ounce of support throughout the ordeal. Every time she found him staked out in front of the window or witnessed him belting out the door, keys in hand, she would insist he was obsessed and needed to find something else to do. But he couldn't think what that might be. His column inches had already shrunk to half of what he'd been allowed a year earlier. His friends had dwindled due to financial issues, relocation or – in a couple of cases – untimely death. Almost everything he had achieved in life had arrived of its own accord. He had made a career out of being the man in the right place and had no idea how to initiate something himself. The battle for the parking space had given him a sense of purpose that he hadn't even realised had gone missing, if it ever existed at all.

In the month following his triumph over Farash, he felt a definite sense of anticlimax. The hell Farash had put him through had lost its bite, and he barely looked over at the King of Kashmir any more. It ceased to exist for him. But he did notice when the restaurant remained in darkness for a few days. The Farash family were presumably still there since the lights were on in the upstairs flat. Not long after this observation, a 'To Let' sign appeared in the window and then, the same week, wreaths and bouquets of flowers were laid in the doorway.

Initially, Dominic assumed these were tributes from loyal customers mourning the loss of the business but when he crossed the street to read some of the cards, he discovered that the king himself was dead. Neighbourhood gossip later revealed he had hung himself in the kitchen.

Dominic hardly had time to process this unintended tragedy when a member of the press, a hungry young hack, turned up at his door. He was a friend of Farash's son, whose name was Pran. Dominic had stood his ground, insisting that he'd dined there, booked under a pseudonym and hedged on the actual date of his booking. But the restaurant evidently had CCTV monitoring that not only revealed he hadn't been there, but had captured him hovering in the doorway as he copied down the blackboard menu.

The headline read 'Critic Buries Chef'. Other papers picked it up, then current affairs television and, after that, life spiralled into chaos. His contract was cancelled. His reputation in tatters. Susannah, who had known nothing of the review (never bothering to follow his work) spent her days railing against him and weeping helplessly. Even after the papers lost interest, he was a pariah in his own street. It seemed impossible that Farash had garnered such loyalty. People who previously greeted Dominic as a local now rejected his custom. Friends not only did *not* commiserate but failed to return his calls, presumably for fear of contamination. He felt like a prisoner in his own home, drinking the day away. So when Susannah suggested they escape to France, it wasn't as though there was anything more appealing on the horizon, and so he agreed.

Now, ironically, he is once again a prisoner in his own home. This time drinking the night away. His destiny, so it seems. This is where it will end.

Drinking at a steady pace, he continues to load up his system. All appreciation is lost, the wine tastes sour and poisonous. Somewhere between the fourth and fifth bottle, he will lapse into unconsciousness. Inevitably organ failure will occur and he will be done for. The most surprising aspect of the whole fiasco is his sense of inebriated equanimity. He can already feel himself fading, and it's not at all disagreeable. He has lived in the best of times, and has no desire to face the worst of times. He feels a sense of peace and satisfaction in the knowledge that he will be remembered. His memoir will outlive him. His words will be read, his story shared, his name uttered long after he has gone.

Chapter Thirty-nine

It's late August when Susannah returns to Cordes-sur-Ciel. As she walks the dogs up the rue Albert Bouquillon towards the Tinkers' house, she has a vivid recollection of the sense of hope she felt that first time she visited. It's almost impossible to believe that so much has happened in less than a year. She has thought often of the Tinkers, always with remorse and guilt. There is no doubt in her mind that her and Dominic's contribution to their lives was nothing but destructive and she half expects to find the place for sale and the Tinkers gone.

Strangely enough, she does miss Dominic a little. These days, she remembers the early years of their relationship more clearly, a time when he did make her laugh, when he was still a wonderful raconteur – before he became a crashing bore. Her memory has begun to play odd tricks, compressing time, changing her perspective. Now she sees their life together as a composite, not just the last years that were marred by anger and arguments, with such a terrible, tragic ending.

Dominic's imprisonment and death was almost like an

elaborate suicide plan, but exactly how it occurred has never fully been established. It was probably as simple as him going down for a bottle of wine, forgetting that he didn't have the key and closing the door. The keys were on the table. He could have found them fairly easily. Unless he went down at night. But why he closed the door, when he normally left it open, she will never know. It was fortunate that she had left the keys behind. The police accepted her version of events that when she left the house, Dominic was still asleep in the living room. The final conclusion was that his imprisonment was accidental.

It was a full month before he was found. Arriving back in London, she had initially been caught up with settling herself into Reggie's little house and being enfolded back into the family. Dominic didn't call that week, which was a little surprising. He obviously knew the phone was on because he took that call from Michelle. Susannah didn't think too much about it during the first week. Knowing him, he probably thought she'd have a change of heart. In retrospect, he would have been absolutely livid at her taking the car and badgering her to return it. By the end of the second week, she began to feel unsettled. Becky thought she was worrying too much. 'He's probably been pissed since you left,' she'd said. How right she was.

Susannah began to phone him at different times of the day and the silence grew eerie. There was that injury to his head. He could have had a stroke. She was determined not to involve the Tinkers again and the Van den Bergs were still away, so there was no one in the village who would be willing to check on him.

Another week passed before Becky acknowledged that perhaps something was awry. Simon had a conference to attend in Geneva, so he agreed to fly via Toulouse on the way back, hire a car and drive to Cordes-sur-Ciel.

Simon had let himself into the house with Susannah's key and realised immediately that something was very wrong. The table was covered in the rotting remains of Christmas lunch. In the kitchen, pots and baking dishes from the meal were stacked unwashed and putrid in the sink. He searched the house thoroughly and finally made his way down to the cellar. He found the two keys on the table in the alcove. He only needed to open the door a crack to know he had found Dominic. Gagging uncontrollably, he walked into the garden and breathed the fresh air. Even so, his lungs seemed to retain some microbes from the stench of the cellar that remained in his nasal passages for hours afterwards. He alerted the *gendarmerie*, cancelled his onward flight and called Becky to break the news.

The temperature of the cellar meant that, although he'd been dead for weeks, Dominic's body was relatively well-preserved. Simon organised cleaners to come through the place and made arrangements for the body to be flown back to London.

Her brother-in-law's response to the situation had changed Susannah's view of him. He'd always seemed stuffy and judgemental, but now she saw a kinder version of him. He was solicitous and efficient, taking responsibility for what needed to be done without complaint. He had returned to the house a month later and had the entire cellar packed up and sent to auction. He appointed a local *immobilier* and put the property up for sale but, so far, not a single prospective buyer had made an enquiry.

It was Becky who suggested that they bring Reggie down for a few days to enjoy the French countryside. Susannah had no desire to return but felt she didn't have much choice. If she was ever going to visit, this was the easiest scenario with her family around her. It was time to make peace with the place. And now it was time to make peace with the Tinkers.

The house on rue Albert Bouquillon looks much the same. The shutters are all open so clearly it is inhabited at least. With some trepidation, she walks up the steps and rings the bell. The door is opened by a small boy. Susannah greets him but he replies in French and runs off, leaving her standing on the doorstep. She realises with regret that the Tinkers have gone, and the child has run off to fetch a parent. So she's all the more surprised when Ben appears. He does an exaggerated double take when he sees her and greets her warmly.

'Come on in!' he says. 'I'm sorry we haven't been in touch, we didn't know where to find you.' He crouches down for a moment and greets the pugs, rubbing their heads affectionately.

Two more children cross the entrance hall and run up the stairs, chatting and laughing. As soon as she steps inside, Susannah notices a different energy in the house, a sense of industry and the sound of distant voices.

'Oh, goodness, you don't need to apologise, Ben. I'm the one who ran away in the night.'

'Probably the only sensible thing to do, the way things went,' he says. 'I did come to check on you the next day but the car had gone and there was no answer. We thought you'd both left. I'm really sorry about Dominic. The story was everywhere online. Some pretty ugly headlines.'

'Yes, I imagine that "Roxy" did very nicely out of it; talk about good timing. Although, if he hadn't shut her in there . . . anyway, I've been over it too many times trying to make sense of it all.'

'Come and see Mia. She'll be really pleased to see you – we've wondered about you. It's a bit crazy at the moment. We're running our first summer art camp, and the place is crawling with kids.'

He takes her through to the long room at the back of the house that opens onto the garden. Even before they reach the room, she can hear young voices twittering like birds. The last time she saw Mia in this room, it was in the dead of winter. The table was covered in the musty old books and records. Mia had seemed dwarfed by the scale of the room, as though she were existing in the shadows between present and past.

Today this room is a world away from that one. The French windows are wide open, the sun pours in and a dozen children sit around the long table chattering and laughing. The table is covered in piles of paper, jars of coloured pencils and plastic tubs of paints. Colourful paintings are pegged up to dry. The children are supervised by a young woman who Ben introduces as Chloe, someone Susannah vaguely remembers seeing around the village. One by one, the children notice the pugs. Jumping up from the table, they gather around, kneeling down to pat the dogs and exclaiming to each other excitedly.

Ben tells them, '*Ils s'appellent Lou-Lou et Chou-Chou.*'

The children rush around, urging the pugs to follow them, calling out, '*Lou-Lou et Chou-Chou, venez ici!* Come! come!' Chloe steps in to quieten them down, ushering them back to the table.

When Mia comes in from the garden, Susannah sees that she is quite transformed. Golden from the sun, her face, always so tight and anxious, has softened. Her body moves with relaxed ease. It is as though she has come into herself. The realisation brings tears to Susannah's eyes.

'Susannah! How are you?' Mia rushes over and hugs her tightly, then picks up both dogs at once and fusses over them. 'Are you back for good?'

'Just for a week or so – the house is being sold, but my family thought we might as well enjoy it in the meantime.'

Ben grimaces. 'How do you feel about that?'

'I wasn't keen at first, as you can imagine. But it's all right. I won't be going down to the cellar, obviously. It's empty now, anyway. All the wine is sold . . . Mia, I'm so sorry I involved you . . .'

Mia puts an arm around her shoulder. 'I'm so sorry about everything that happened. I'm glad I could help you. I think you were incredibly brave.'

Susannah thinks of Dominic's pages curling to ash in the fireplace and has to agree, she had been braver than she ever thought possible.

'Will you stay for coffee? Come out into the garden. I'm so glad you're here,' says Mia.

Ben excuses himself; he has a class underway upstairs. While Mia fetches the coffee, Susannah goes out to the garden. As she settles herself under the canopy of the chestnut tree she realises that, although she hasn't known the Tinkers long, they have witnessed a period of her life that will forever be impossible to explain. To say you had to be there doesn't begin to cover it. She feels overwhelming relief that the Tinkers survived it – and, despite it all, have flourished.

She too has survived, and even begun to bloom a little. She has settled into life with Reggie and adjusted to his routines. Had she returned from France in the state she was in and found herself living alone for the first time in her life, it could have been the end of her.

Through her own endeavour, she has secured a position as sales assistant in a little homewares shop within walking distance of the house. Thanks to work, and the structure of life in Reggie's world, for the first time she can recall, there is something firm to hold on to after so many years of feeling that everything was slipping away from her grasp. She lives a life of quiet anonymity, for which she is deeply grateful.

When Mia returns with coffee and butter cake, they pick up where they left off. Susannah has a strong feeling that her relationship with Mia, forged in fire, will endure where others have fallen away.

Mia explains it was Chloe, the woman from the art shop, who gave her the idea for a summer camp. 'I knew straight away that this was the perfect project for us. It had all the right ingredients. I knew we could make it work.'

It seems they have a dozen children attend every day during the school holidays. Chloe's mother is also involved, preparing a hot lunch for the students, which is apparently standard. 'We're starting small and hopefully we'll expand to a residential summer camp for children and perhaps artist retreats for overseas visitors. Still in the planning, so we'll see how it goes. We'll close over winter and head back home for Christmas.'

'Wonderful! I think it's all just wonderful. Ben's French has obviously improved too,' says Susannah with a smile.

'It's had to.' Mia laughs. 'He's still got a long way to go but he's running our *École des Passionnés d'informatique* – Geek School – teaching kids how to code. The older ones learn English at school, so they meet somewhere in the middle. I don't know how he gets by, but he does.'

'I'm so glad you've made it work. And so thrilled you're still here. I told you the sun would shine eternal for you,' says Susannah. And as she looks around the garden and back towards the house, full of sun and children, she realises that the Tinkers have found their *raison d'être*. They have breathed new life into this house and it has offered them a new life in return.

She wonders whether she will find something truly worthwhile to do with her time. A purpose. A reason for being. She had always thought of herself as helpless and a bit incompetent – a view that was reflected by those around her. The events of this last year have proved otherwise. The idea of being alone and entirely responsible for herself has always terrified her. Now she is discovering that she can stare into that abyss and see beyond the darkness. There is a faint glow in the distance, and as she moves towards it she knows it will become brighter and expand around her and she will be comforted by it. She will step into the light on her own. It will be her light. And she is determined to walk towards it every day.

Chapter Forty

Ben and I came to France in the hope that relocating would somehow restore our faith in ourselves and each other. We couldn't accept that we had both changed. Everything we didn't want to accept, everything too painful to discuss, was packed away, out of sight. Ben couldn't face my sorrow; I couldn't see the hidden depths of his disappointment.

In the weeks after that terrible Christmas Day, we circled around each other. I didn't have any plans and didn't dare ask about his. Ben went back to work and I barely saw him. I walked the winter days away and would often find myself standing, gazing into the distance, seeing nothing. Waiting for something to change. The French don't say I miss you, they say *tu me manques* — more like, you are missing from me. Ben was missing from me.

The news of Dominic's death changed everything. Ben was horrified by the thought of his lonely end, imprisoned in that dark cellar. Ben had gone to the house on Boxing Day, knocked at the door, walked around the outside of house. Now he wondered if he had heard someone calling. Did Dominic know he was there? He had probably been Dominic's only hope of rescue.

He was completely devastated. It was as if all his buried grief rose to the surface and gushed out. We spent hours discussing the circumstances surrounding Dominic's death and once we started talking, we didn't stop. We began to get to the heart of our own stuff. It was painful and upsetting. We cried and we argued. We listened to each other's truth and I finally came to realise that, up until the time of our crisis, my life had been a golden one. I was a stranger to adversity and I didn't cope well. I had sabotaged our life together because I couldn't get what I wanted and didn't know how to deal with that. Ben is the grounded one and he pulled me back to earth. In life, Dominic had divided us but his death reunited us.

By the time that bitter winter turned to spring, Ben and I were growing back together. Around the entire perimeter of the house, strong green stems pushed their way up. Pods formed at the centre of each and the petals peeled back to reveal a perfect orange or gold crown inside; each a corona in a constellation of daffodils, nodding and dancing with the breeze.

The dark ploughed fields sprouted bright-green barley. Wildflowers in pinks and blues and yellows threaded their way through the fields. The stark outlines of trees softened with blossom. The village itself woke from hibernation, kitchen chairs were brought outside to catch the morning sun, and people greeted each other with a new lightness.

Chloe's husband, Marc, speaks English and we began to spend time with them and their two children. One evening over dinner, Chloe talked about the difficulties of running her business during all the school holidays, eight weeks during the summer alone. As is traditional all over France, their boys are sent away to *colonies de vacances* – holiday camp. As I listened, the pieces of our puzzle began to slide into place. Our huge house. My love of art and teaching. Children to fill the silent rooms, just as Madame Levant had hoped. And so the first seeds of our venture were sown that night. As it turns out, the four of us have the perfect skill set for this little business. Marc works in the public service and could navigate the complicated bureaucracy for the permits we needed. Ben is our IT expert and Chloe is part of a whole community of artists and artisans – painters, ceramicists, leatherworkers, jewellers – people we can involve in future ventures.

Sometimes I still have dreams about the child I thought we would have. It's a nostalgic dream of lost love but I sense that loss is like any other scar – it will fade with time. I don't put my energies into that longing any more. I had to let go of my dream child to share my life with many children. To be awake to the living world.

Only a few months ago, we lived here in isolation hearing the children pass by every day. Now we have the chance to become part of the village and the children are a part of our lives. We don't know how long we'll stay – maybe a few years, maybe longer, maybe forever. But one thing I do know: Ben is here for me. And I am here for him.

Acknowledgements

Special thanks to all those who provided invaluable background information, support and considered feedback on early versions of the manuscript: Milan Wynyard, Tula Wynyard, Joseph Furolo, Tracey Trinder, Carolinda Witt, Catherine Hersom-Bowens, Laurence Clary, Helen Thurloe, David Parker, Richard Woolveridge, Marianne Hurzeler-Schranz, Fritha Borland, Jan and Murray Turnbull, Christianne Zeelen and Nico Thomassen.

As always, a big thank you to the fabulous team at Penguin Random House: Ali Watts, Saskia Adams, Amanda Martin, Nerrilee Weir, Chloe Davies and Louise Ryan.

Book Club Discussion Notes

1. Which of the characters did you relate to the most?

2. What was your favourite moment in the novel?

3. Do you think Susannah did the right thing leaving without telling Dominic?

4. Could Susannah have stood up for herself earlier and made the marriage work?

5. Was it a good decision for Mia and Ben to escape to France and another life?

6. Do you think Dominic was an egotist and a narcissist, or simply a product of his time?

7. Did Ben's struggle to adapt to life in France highlight some of the potential difficulties of moving to a foreign country?

8. If you had the opportunity to live in another country for a few years, would you take it? Where would you go?

9. In what ways did the setting contribute to the story?

10. Do you think the book was character driven, or plot driven? Why?

11. Did your opinion of any of the characters change over the course of the story, and how?

12. What did you think about the dynamics between the characters?

13. If you were casting the film, who would you cast as Susannah and Dominic?

14. Do the themes of this book relate to any of the author's other books? In what ways?

Discover a
new favourite